I0562978

WHEN GODS FALL I

Nelson Lowhim

Also By Nelson Lowhim

When Gods Fail III

Tree of Freedom

The Struggle Trilogy

CityMuse

Rebel

Alternative Book Press
2 Timber Lane
Suite 301
Marlboro, NJ 07746
www.alternativebookpress.com

This is a work of fiction. All characters appearing in this work are fictitious.
Any resemblance to real people, living or dead or otherwise, or locales is
purely coincidental.

2013 Paperback Edition
Copyright 2013 © Nelson Lowhim
Cover Illustration by Nelson Lowhim
Book Design by Nelson Lowhim
All rights reserved
Published in the United States of America by Alternative Book Press

Originally published in electronic form in the United States by Eiso
Publishing.
Library of Congress Cataloging-in-Publication Data

Nelson, Lowhim, [date]
When Gods Fail II/ by Nelson, Lowhim.—1st ed.
p. cm.
1. Science—Fiction (Fiction). I Title.
PN1-6790-380.L69W446   2013
813'.6—dc23
2013945014

ISBN 978-1-940122-07-6
Printed in the United States of America
10 9 8 7 6 5 4 3 2 1

Thou shalt not live, for thou speakest lies in the name of the Lord.
-The Bible

Table of Contents:

I burn the entire thing. Bill's place, as I now call it. With some of the fuel they'd saved up, I dose the shipping container, make sure the trap door is open, then toss a match onto a gasoline-soaked canvas which hangs out the trapdoor. I nestle myself in a place between two rocks, on the foot of a nearby hill, some hundred yards away.

It's beautiful; the flames lick up from the trapdoor and soon the entire shipping container is engulfed in this torrent of flames. I feel the heat on my face. The smell of various plastics and clothes burning hit my nostrils. My body relaxes, and with the odd carbon-like smells, I feel like I am at a campfire. It's still evening.

A small explosion rips the side of the shipping container. A piece of shrapnel whistles by me, and I move so that there's a rock between the container and me.

I take my eyes off the flames and look around. I should have climbed higher. Half the reason behind burning this place was to see if it attracted anyone. No, you're lying to yourself again. There's one real reason you're doing this.

Her.

That's right, she's gone. Couldn't bear the sight of me anymore, and decided to take her life instead. Just the thought of that last moment—her eyes looking at me like I was a stain—it grips my heart and shakes my body.

I buried her body a week ago. Dug a grave as deep as I could, then threw her body in, wrapped with her clothes. All her clothes and almost anything that could be remotely considered hers. I once thought that certain traditions required, or needed, someone to be buried with their artifacts from this life because of some hope of an afterlife. Now I see it differently. There's a desire, even for a woman I'm sure I love or loved, to get rid of the deceased person's things so that they didn't infect everything you do.

I'll sleep alone tonight. No more touch, no more warmth, no more her. Wasn't she the new reason for me? Wasn't she all that mattered? She was. And she is no more. I cry.

When the shipping container finally falls on itself, the hungry fire eating everything worth eating, the sun is setting. The days are getting brighter, with the clouds lifting little by little. It's a hopeful sign, but I can't take heart with all that had happened. I feel nothing. And here I am burning the place that *she* told me I shouldn't. She'd said that it would be counter to my idea of building a new world, but what did she care about that?

I focus on the horizon, a darkening outline that will soon be a landscape devoid of life, like it's always been. I hope that some people out there will see the fire, the billowing smoke.

It doesn't happen; as night collapses all around me, and embers of the fire heave like a giant creature trying to escape its prison, I hear nothing but the stillness of the wasteland I now know is my home. Not even the insects—that I know live underground, that are now making a meal of Jenny's corpse—make a peep. The silence grows, a few pops and crackles from the embers, and when that dies out, when the darkness comes upon me, there is nothing to listen to but the sound of my shoes grinding on dirt, my heart in my ribcage, and a whine in my ears. It's soft at first, yet the more the silence of the land smothers me, the more this piercing siren tickles my ear drums.

Another shiver comes over me, and I stand up and move to the cave. Slow tortuous movements that make certain I don't scrape myself on the rocks or fall needlessly. On the top of my hill I look down and try to see the remnants of the fire. There is nothing. If someone's to find the place they'll only spot a few ashes. The news about how the world ended, a possible shelter for someone in need, is now gone. The act was futile, and I know it.

I lie down in my cave and think about the next few days. I roll Jenny's image in my mind, trying to somehow knead her into a different shape. It's to no avail. I wonder if I'm finally going mad. Humans are social creatures are they not? And I have *no one*.

There's only quiet nothingness. Not just of the night, but of knowing that there's nothing out there. Everything's destroyed; I know this. So the silence isn't some freak occurrence that'll be broken by a plane, or a person, or a car driving by. No, it will be there for as long as I'm around, and when I die it will get louder. In fact that I'm here is a violation of this new quiet law. I sense a suffocation from these thoughts, and I hold my breath for as long as I can, just to see if it'll work, if the silence will penetrate my cavity, still my heart and all my other organs, and choke me to death so that the world is quiet again.

And in this nothingness, in this world where the quiet is a killer waiting to get me, where I am an aberration in the laws of nature, Jenny comes to me. Not an image, though I try my hardest to get an image of her sensuous body, but a glimpse of her eyes before she jumped, or rather the feeling of disgust it invoked in me. I hate myself for what she made me feel, especially at the end of her life. And since I can also compare it to the elation I felt, when we had sex— once—when she seemed to like me and with that mere acceptance was able to set my entire being on fire, I find that it hurts that much more.

Why Jenny? Why did you leave?

A tear falls from my cheek as I look at these feelings that she pulled out of me, these substitutions of what hope once looked like, and I try to think of where things could've gone wrong. But there hasn't been an answer since I first asked this question.

My hand runs over the ground in front of me, and I come across a ring. I pick it up. It's hers. What's it doing here? The ring is warm in my hand, and I slip it on my right pinkie finger. It does nothing. That empty, horrid, feeling is still there, and there are no answers. Like the strangling quiet, this feeling that Jenny evokes, *evoked* in me, threatens to end me. Between the two I'm not certain which one will get me first. I ask another question: what should I do? And again I'm met by silence. I want to scream. Fire all my ammunition into this silence, and maybe into the feeling. I pull out my handgun and point it at my chest. That's where it hurts the most; that is where some disease Jenny gave me is eating my heart. And yet even when I think there is no hope, I don't pull the trigger. Why?

Again the silence answers.

The ringing in my ears.

My heart beats.

I hold my breath.

Nothing.

It's times like these when I wonder how the first caveman could've been religious. How could he have stood against the nothingness and imagined that something was out there? I'm certain that nothing is in fact out there, but I am also frightened of this thinking. Frightened that if I look too deep inside I'll find something I don't like. If I stay away, or don't poke too deep, I can be sad from a distance. If I go up close. Who knows?

I wake up still tired. I feel is relief that I'm finally up and away from the dreams. I have hints of running, of jumping, of sex. Of rape. I think. The images fade away. I put on my shoes; dark leather boots I took from Bill's body, and that fit well. The day is well on its way by the time I stick my head out the cave's entrance. I see cracks in the sky, even a few holes, but there's no improvement. In time, I think to myself. I climb to the peak directly above the cave. With my handgun hidden underneath my new coat, or rather Bill's, and a shotgun in hand, I try to make out if any footprints or smells have appeared around the area. Nothing.

I get to the top. My heart starts to warn me by bouncing against my ribcage. I feel hairs stand up and I turn, my back to the cliff edge. I crouch down, trying to take deep breaths. What's so wrong about this place? Perhaps the fact that Jenny jumped from here? I know I don't believe in ghosts, and yet her touch and smell is somewhere here, or somewhere in my brain's deep recesses, somewhere my conscious can never hope to touch. Or perhaps an enemy lurks somewhere. I do have the same feeling as before we saw those men, me and Jenny.

I remember reading about this: that the adrenaline gland tends to react the same for both. Science. It was meant to answer all our questions and yet here I am, alone with nothing, and all I can think of is how useless it was in saving us from ourselves.

A crack echoes across the land. I'm not alone! I strain my eyes and see no movement. The noise disappears.

I drop to my ass and look over the edge of the cliff. The bottom is far down; my brain wants to jump over while also screaming at me to stay away. Die... live. I try to make myself believe that this is not the way it's always been, that I'm of a state of mind whereby I'm willing to die because of the nothingness that surrounds me.

And yet my memory speaks up, and I know that this is not so. I remember being a child with my parents, faint shadows of authority, yelling at me as I pretended to be a ballerina on the ledge of the roof on our ten-story building. I looked down and saw the ground so far and so tempting, as if a fall would only be flight, and that's what called me as a child, that moment to fly if only for a second, and while part of my brain was thrilled another part knew what I'd been told: that this was dangerous that this was the way to die because the air ends at some point and there is ground, and the ground will punch you so hard that you die, and I balanced these two in my head as my parents rushed to me, grab me, told me to never do that again.

And here I am now, an adult, staring at the abyss, the thrill of flying acts as a loud chorus, and I realize that nothing has changed, that I feel the same way as I ever did, that I perhaps was always tainted with this insane ability. I push myself back from the edge. Was this what called Jenny? Did she feel the need to fly for a moment?

I wonder.

If so, why is anyone made so that we are constantly battling between what's good for us and what can kill us? Treating each like they're equal, when in any reasonable view they're not? Is that what got us into this mess? Did the men who had the nuclear buttons, before they pressed them, look at the button and feel the same as I do today? I think of a quote by a survivor of the nuclear bombs in Japan, one of the few, who said the person who controls the option for using a nuclear weapon, should be a pregnant woman. No one took him seriously, when they very well should've. Maybe pregnant women don't have two voices cheering them on as they sit next to a cliff.

My throat tightens. An organism destined to be wiped out, like lemmings that decide to run over cliffs to prevent over-population. And we were supposed to be saved by our innovation. What good was innovation when we always had those two voices in our heads? I pick up a rock and throw it over the edge. This is the way of things, I tell myself.

And *you* did it to her, it wasn't the two voices, don't lie to yourself, *you* did it to her.

Another screech sounds across the land. I hold my breath and scan the land around me. Nothing. My mind is full of such noises.

I think of her staring at the place where I took her virginity. But she kissed me back. *I know she did.*

What choice did you give her? I'd never really dwelt on that night, what my thoughts were. It frightened me. With her I was supposed to save the human race.

What a fool you were.

But she kissed me back.

You fool.

Light headed, I pick up another rock and throw it over.

After that night, when she saw me kill that boy...

You were cruel.

But how'd others wanted to kill me on sight.

Does that excuse it? If you were supposed to rule the world with her, then she was your rightful judge and you were judged a monster, admit it.

I think of her eyes, soft, the moment where she looked at me with a look of care, and then that final look.

A tear falls down my cheek. I bring my knees to my chest and hug my thighs. The cliff seems to be calling me. I can't.

Why not? What else is there?

There has to be something else. Humans cannot go out so quietly, can they?

I take in the land, it's still desolate, still no sign of another human.

I get up from my seat of rocks, ignore the voice and walk down to the cave. I have Bill and Paul's sled. I fill it with rations, manuals and ammunition. I will start the long walk back to the place where I ran into the men. I'll meet the family I spared and ask them for forgiveness. Then I'll lay my hands at their mercy. If they feel that I deserve none, I'll accept it. I just need to be around people.

I sleep without tossing or turning in my bed. I don't even think of Jenny. Just the short pang of loneliness and the anticipation of meeting people again. Sure there's the risk of getting into another fight, but being alone in this desolate landscape is worse.

The next day I take the sled and head out. I make certain that the cave's entrance's still hidden. I scatter rocks so that if they're moved I'll know, and I make certain that the trip wires and booby traps, things I learned from Bill's manual, are in place and ready to go.

What will I say to the family? I'll have to deny killing the other men in their family. And yet do I want to start things out on the wrong foot? New beginning, right?

When I saw the family, I thought them friendly. But wasn't that something I saw in the mother? Bill? Each person I met, I decided to see some sort of goodness in them...

Don't be foolish. Do you want to stay alone in that cave? Allow Jenny's ghost to come after you?

I tell myself these things over and over as I walk to the family's abode. I keep an eye out for signs of life, for enemies lurking, but I see nothing. I smell nothing. The nothingness creeps into my body. I sleep out in the open, away from the rocks. I don't know why. I feel like if my time has come, it'll come. The sun sets. The sky is an unfortunate purple.

I think of how Jenny saved me with her shot. Then how she couldn't take that she'd *ended* someone. That was it. She didn't survive. And so her way of life wouldn't go on. You cold bastard. You just want to make yourself feel better.

When I wake up I'm startled by a noise. It's morning and the shadows around me are small. I grab my two handguns and point them at a couple rocks. Then around me. My hair prickles my skin, and I wonder what it could be. For a second I think mutations, comic book style, with deformed beings who know nothing of love and affection and only of eating their next meal. What if bullets can't stop them?

I strain to hear. A dream. I eat my breakfast, more military rations, and set out. It's not long before I come to the natural alleyway where I ran into those men with Jenny.

When I get to the bodies they're still there. No flesh. The insects have picked them clean. It's kind of amazing. And horrific. I look up at the walls to either of my side. Nothing. I look over to the bodies. Unmoved. Why?

I'm glad that I changed my boots with Bill. It means that the imprints from my previous shoes, used in this shooting, will not match up to the footprints I make now.

When I get close to the divot between the two peaks, I leave my sled and sit down to listen. I can hear the young girl playing a game and laughing. Laughter. It's been a while. My heart lurches. I step forward and stop myself.

The men I shot had been hostile. There was no reason to believe that this family wasn't the same.

I stuff a handgun in my pants, hidden, then another under my coat. There's no use trying to live in this world alone, or trying to travel to Central America alone.

When I arrive at the shacks, everything is quiet.

"Hello? Is anyone here?" I yell out. "Hello?"

The fluids in my body race around, faster and faster, and all I can hear, again, is me—the aberration in this world. The warmth that will, sooner or later, lose out to its surroundings and will become one with it, and I will no longer exist; same thing will happen to the earth, its warm gooey center will freeze, the sun too will go dormant, and then the galaxy, as the sheet of the universe stretches everything to nothing and the whole damn thing comes to a halt. Knowing this, I still want to go forward; I'm still risking my life so that I can feel a little affection from the touch of another human. Knowing all this, I am a born fool.

"Hello," I yell out again. I can feel the tension in my voice. There can be someone in those shacks, perhaps a ledge I haven't noticed above me, with a rifle and bead on me, waiting to pull the trigger, making sure that they don't make the mistake of letting a stranger, who could very well kill them, near them.

I hold out my hands above my chest. I feel light all over, thinking about being shot like this, here in the middle of trying to be nice one more time. "I'm here to talk. Please. Come out. I am not here to fight."

Nothing. I'm certain that I heard the girl earlier, but now there isn't the slightest movement. I let out some air. What if they don't want to see me or meet me? What if they just want to be left alone?

"Hello?"

I hear the squirming of a girl. Then a cough. It isn't loud, but with my ears poised for anything, with all the quiet that preceded it, it sounds like a shot. It comes from the shack. I take a step forward, then decide that it would be foolish to approach them. They're obviously trying to stay quiet.

"I can hear you. Trust me. Please," I say the last word with as much masculinity stripped from my voice as possible. "If you want me to leave, never come back. Just tell me. All right?"

I wait for a few heartbeats. "Can you at least tell me that much?"

I think about what I would do if they sent me away. This possibility seems much more horrifying than getting into a shootout with them. It would signify the end of trying to meet other people. That's not the only thing, though. The voice, that animal in me, the one I am trying to hold down and keep quiet speaks up: and in a world like this, don't turn your back on them, they will shoot you. You think they can't put the disappearance of their friends and the appearance of you together?

I can't listen to that voice, the one that did *that* to Jenny. Be smart; convince them.

"I understand that you're worried about my intentions," I say as I raise my hands above my head. "Look. Nothing. I come only to look for someone to talk to. There's no one else. I just lost my wife." I speak of Jenny, as well as Carol, and hold my breath. "I'm heading south, and all I want is someone to talk to. Please."

The wind picks up.

"All right then. I'll leave."

I turn my back and hear movement. I spin back around, reaching for my handgun.

"Easy," says the man I saw earlier, who's stepped out of the shack; a rifle's in his hands, but it isn't pointed at me.

"You scared me."

"I know. I'm sorry about that." His eyes dart around.

"I didn't expect to see anyone here," I say, wondering where his daughter is. "Or at least to come out. May I?"

"I'll come up there."

He walks up to me, and we shake hands. A firm grip, this is what I am looking for. Don't relax too much, the voice said.

"Tom," I say, smiling.

"I'm James." He nods and smiles, though it seems to pain him when he does so.

He's holding the rifle by the butt stock, it swings, and I feel that he's relaxed enough that I look away, scan what's around us.

"I have food," I say, though I'm not certain why. I made my case earlier and now I want him to do some of the heavy lifting. At least he hasn't tried to blow my brains out.

He nods, though he seems confused by my words. That makes two. He has light skin that is red with a tinge of olive hinting at some exotic background. Everything else about him isn't that impressive. He's as skinny as I am; his flesh hangs confidently off his bones. He has the air of a father who is only looking for the next meal for his child. His eyes continuously dart everywhere. In a way they remind me of Paul's, though kinder.

"That's good," he replies after a long pause.

I try to look at his eyes, blue rings, but I look at his blemishes instead. There are old scars over his forearms and cheeks.

"It is," I say. There's tension between us, like a whole other person between us. Yet there isn't much I can say to make this better is there? Everything feels odd, and even though I'm acting weird by all measures, he's acting odd too, and it feels natural too.

Then I remember that I should mention the bodies. No need trying to deny it, as sooner or later he'll see that I pulled my sled by them. "I saw some bodies down that way." I point past the peak. "There many people around here?"

He tenses up. He stops swinging the rifle. "Who were they?"

I shrug. "Don't know. Four bodies. Picked clean by... the wind I suppose," I say.

"Insects," he says, a little too assured a manner for my likes. "Insects pick the bodies apart.

"Oh," I say, though I think that he sees through my lie.

"The flesh at least."

I nod my head. I'm a little scared of him, of how easily he's talking about insects eating human flesh.

"You been alone ever since the bombs?" I ask, wanting to tell him every little detail about my life about how I feel.

I sense that he doesn't like the alone question. His gaze rests in one place, and he tenses up. I suppose in a situation like this it would seem like a question about capabilities, wouldn't it?

"I mean, I'm alone right now. Lost my wife, like I said. It hurts, being alone. The world the way it is." I feel relieved. I look him in his eyes; they seem calm. Will this be what he believes?

"I see," he says, the tension leaving his body.

There's no way to know if he sees this weakness on my part as a thing to reach and befriend, or as something to take advantage of.

"You said you were heading south?"

"I am. Or I will, at least. I saw that there were people here, and I was ecstatic. You know?"

"I'm sure," he says. The balance of tension and trust and calm seem like they are in perfect harmony inside him.

"I figure that places in Central America and the Amazon couldn't have been touched. Right? So that's why I'm heading down there. Plus the weather will be warmer. Winter will be here soon and that'll make living pretty hard."

His face cracks a smile, and I see wrinkles form all across it like a hidden network. He's older than I thought.

"You're going all the way to Central America?" He laughs as he says this. "You know where we are, right?"

There isn't anything condescending in his voice, he's genuinely amused by my mission. Now that I think about it, it seems a little far-fetched.

"I'm alone. What would you have me do? Live the rest of my days in a cave?"

He twists his head and face. "No, I guess I would try everything to find someone."

The wind picks up, pushes the air between us.

"Where were you when this all went down?" I ask.

He looks me over and up to the sky. The clouds have cracks and rays streaking down like shafts. Perhaps there'll be some weather soon.

"I'm a geologist. Was," he says. "My family came out here to visit me on an excavation. Pure luck, really. We were below ground when it hit. Most of the people on my team were off in town getting supplies. The few here were exposed." He shakes his head. "Horrendous thing, seeing a man with his eyes peeling, blind, groping, hoping to die with some dignity." He stares at my chest like a ghost is growing out of it.

I imagine men or women or children groping around in this place, radiation exposure making their survival impossible. I want to ask what he did with them, then decide that it won't be for the best. What he did he had to do. I wouldn't want someone making judgments on me, would I? Besides, he mentioned his family, though it might have been a slip.

"You?" he asks, his rifle switches hands, though he makes sure that it doesn't once point at me.

"You probably won't believe it, but I was spelunking, in some caves north of here. I was deep in exploration when some earthquakes hit. I thought, at least." James seems to be taking my story at face value, and when I finish telling him about how I got out and what I saw, he shook his head.

"So under a rock, eh?"

"Yeah, lucky, I suppose."

"Your wife?"

How do I tell him this? Do I mention Jenny, or do I mention Carol? Does it matter? "I met a woman, a day after I was out. She was alone, and she took me into her place."

Silence envelopes us and for a second I think I hear a bird. I look up, and he does too. "Did you hear that?"

"I heard something, but I don't think there are any birds."

"If we both heard it, then it has to be real, right?" I say.

"No, I've followed a few sounds. It ends up being the wind pushing scraps against a wall or something like that. Just phantom sounds, our brains think in a certain way, so we both heard it, but it doesn't mean anything."

I crane my neck to see the sky. He's right, there's nothing, and if I'm to start chasing sounds I'll simply become a madman.

"Let's go see the bodies you were talking about."

"They people you know?"

He doesn't answer and tips his head to indicate that I should lead. He wants me in front of him, where he can keep an eye on me. Of course this means that I won't be able to see him, and the last thing I want is to give someone in this lawless land an opportunity to shoot me in the back of the head. So I grant him his wish, but walk in front and to the side of him so that I can see him as well. He seems content with this setup and follows me.

We walk past my sled, which he glances over and smiles, saying: "This is what you were gonna drag to Central America?"

"Yep." I grin. My idea now sounds so outlandish that I start to doubt my state of mind.

When we get to the bodies, all appears peaceful. There's no sign, from afar, that these men met a violent end. James walks up to the bodies and one by one inspects them. "Looks like they were here for a while."

"That's my guess."

He looks at me, and I know he's trying to gauge whether I did this or not. After all, if not me who?

"I think they were shot," he says and points to a shattered bone.

"That's my guess too." I walk up to him and try to think of asking some more questions. I stay silent afraid that my nervousness will show through my voice. The fact that he doesn't seem distraught, that in fact he's only observing like a scientist worries me. Does he have any connection to these people? The boy had said that his family was beyond the peak. That means that James has to be that family, correct?

"Will you help me bury them?"

"Of course," I say and guess he knows them, why else would someone want to bury a few strangers?

We head back, unload my sled near the shack area, then bring the bodies back on it. We dig a large shallow grave and lower the bodies into it. I haven't seen the two females from before, so I'm checking my rear constantly. Why else hasn't he introduced me to them? My mind is trying to bring my body back to speed, trying to make sure that it doesn't end up being too relaxed about James. He's burying these bodies without a single tear.

I hear a twig crunch and turn. It comes from inside a shack. I keep James in the corner of my eye. "What was that? More phantoms?"

"No," James says after a long pause. "Honey, come out. It's safe."

Out walk the woman and young girl. The girl has a guilty look on her face.

"I'm sorry daddy," she says, twisting and looking at her shoes.

"That's all right sweetheart, come here."

The girl runs to James, and he puts down his rifle as he picks her up and cradles her across his chest. He's vulnerable, but I take this as him finally trusting me. I stride to the woman I assume is his wife, and shake hands with her. "I'm Tom, pleased to meet you."

"Hi, I'm Samantha." She shakes my hand, and I feel funny as the flash in her eyes reminds me of Jenny.

I turn to make sure that James is in my periphery and notice that he's walking over, his daughter still in his arms.

"You two met already, I see," he says as he pushes the girl forward. "This is Tom honey."

"Hi Tom," the girl says, barely taking a visual lick of me before burying her face in her father's shoulder.

"She's shy. Honey, what do we say?"

She shakes her head, and I wonder what it matters to teach a child things such as manners in this new world. New beginning, I remind myself.

"That's fine."

"Honey." James ignores me and coaxes some words out of his daughter. "Don't be rude to our guest."

She sticks out her hand. "I'm Sarah, pleased to meet you," she says in a hurried tone.

"Pleased to meet you as well."

James puts down Sarah and glances over at the grave. "We'd better finish that."

"Who is it?" Sarah says as she sights the hole in the ground and the bones and clothes sticking above the surface.

"Mark and Tony, honey," James says with a sad tone.

Sarah seems to be struck by the names, then appears to calm down. Has she been desensitized to death? Or perhaps they didn't know them as well as I think.

"Did you know them?" I ask.

James looks at me, as if he cannot make up his mind about something. I start to feel nervous. The fact that sweet little Sarah seems to be matching his demeanor makes me even more nervous. I look at Samantha who also seems to be looking at the bodies with tranquility.

"We knew them. But they were..." James trails off and whispers to himself.

25

I think about the young man. Was it possible that a man would spew lies for his last words? I bite the side of my cheek and the sour blood that is released eases the tension in my guts. Whatever's going on here it seems to be beyond my grasp. I decide to play along, but keep an eye on them.

I help James shovel dirt on the skeletons until they're covered. As we do this, Samantha and Sarah stand to the side, and Sarah mumbles in tongues I cannot understand. My guts tighten back up. Part of me wants to leave now. But I don't want to be alone.

As night comes James starts to put together some objects for a fire.

"Where did you get that?"

"This? I had it for the expedition; it's chemically coated wood chips. Burns forever." He holds it out for me to look at.

I take it in my hand and examine it with more zest than is necessary. I have no clue what it is, but I'm trying to adapt to their little world here.

James points me to their shack. I will sleep on the floor with them. I don't know if he's doing so because he completely trusts me with his family and is willing to have me close by, or if he doesn't trust me and wants to keep an eye on me.

The next day I help them chip at a little rock edifice they have going. I notice that there are some bones at the feet of this odd shape. Are they human? I can't tell the difference. The rock shape they're making is inside a shack that has three walls of plastic siding, the fourth one being the side of the mountain that we are chipping away at. I keep quiet. I feel that I shouldn't interfere with their customs. Sarah's mumblings, as she chips away at the rock, worms into my brain.

I look at Samantha who's building some sort of dolls from old clothes, and she only looks at me, smiles. It isn't the smile of a mother—I assume she's Sarah's mother—who's slightly embarrassed of her daughter's habits, however, it's merely the smile of woman who isn't yet certain about the stranger in her midst. For a second, though, when she turns her back to me and returns to working on the dolls, I look at the curve in her short body; curves that still scintillate even after her obvious weight loss. Blood rushes to my cock, and I look back at the rock face in front of me. I think of Jenny, but mostly I think of Samantha, her smell now filling my lungs, and how nice it would be to have her in my arms.

Willing or not.

And James is outside trying to find rocks that we can also turn into dolls.

I turn back to look at her and absorb that feminine form that now burns itself into my mind, outlines like the sun just setting on a majestic landscape. I turn to Sarah who's looking at me in an odd manner. I channel my focus to the rock face.

I'm sure that she's too young to know what my look really meant. How old was she, after all? Ten, thirteen at the most? I glance over and Sarah stares back at me. There is a tinge of fear in her eyes, and she has stopped mumbling. My eyes roll back to the orange rock. I cannot believe that the thought of taking Samantha, anyway I can, has even entered my mind. After all this, after what I had put Jenny through, I am willing to do it again. It's the voice, some hideous instinct that I cannot merely push away in this landscape. Nevertheless I make a half promise to myself to stay away and control myself. I now have an inkling as to why this family was not so sad to see those men die.

At one point Sarah and Samantha leave the shack. When I walk out of the shack, temple, I see the family together, whispering. It's obvious from the way they tense up in silence, that they're talking about me. Did Sarah divulge what she saw?

James walks off, and Samantha smiles at me again. This time it seems friendly. Remember the mother you tried to save, I think, or not so much think as feel through my balls and bones and only think as a precaution or backstop to becoming a complete animal again.

The sun hides behind the peak and it's dark early in our large natural depression. James lights the fire, and we huddle around it. I pull out some cocoa mix that I have in my backpack and start to boil water over the fire. James has access to a well here, and they don't lack for water. The family looks at the packet I have greedily. I mix the water and the cocoa powder together and pass it to Sarah.

"Try it, it's great."

Sarah looks at me and the brew. I can see she likes the smell.

"Go ahead honey," James says.

Sarah drinks it and smiles, all her teeth exposed, and I smile back. It feels good to do something for someone else. I actually forgot what this felt like.

"It's good," Sarah manages to say as she takes more gulps, torn between swallowing as much of it as possible and savoring it in her mouth.

"Sarah, you have to share," Samantha says.

Sarah looks at her mother and for a moment looks like she will defy her, then softens up. "Sorry."

"That's fine." I wave off their concerns. "I have plenty more of those. It's good, so go ahead." I get up and go to my pile of goodies outside the shack. In a minute I return with several more packets. "See?"

Sarah's eyes gleam. "Can I have more?"

I laugh. "Of course."

"Honey." Jame's voice is tinged with low anger. "Let's not take things from our guests. All right? We can have more for tomorrow." And as James says this, he gives me an appreciative look. I take this to mean: please, we're trying to teach our daughter a little discipline in this world, do you mind helping?

I nod my head and place the packets down by my side. I might be a libertine influence that they want to be rid of. I decide that I shouldn't open up.

It goes like this for almost a week. I help them with a few chores around the small compound, and they keep a friendly but mistrustful eye on me. At night I share a few of my goodies, Sarah being the main consumer, and we hardly talk.

I am entirely not certain what to make of this. It seems against my every instinct not to talk to them. For them, however, it seems like a natural state of being.

And yet inside me the ghosts start to rear their heads. They seem to have grown powerful in the presence of others. I do not mean the violent urges, or sexual compulsion that has gripped me for so long, that I beat down like a chaste monk whenever I see Samantha in some exposed position.

No, I am talking about the need to be careful, the whispers of the mother I killed, how everyone else wanted me killed. That, if this family is not normal when it comes to conversation, then why should I expect them to be normal in other facets of life? I think about what I would do in their situation. Would telling me to move on really be a good decision? If I've even the inkling of a mean streak, I'd only find high ground and shoot them one by one. No, in this world, the only choice is to end any threats. If we cannot be friends, we will be enemies.

In the end, I cannot do much except to wait for their open arms.

One night, Samantha and Sarah head in early as I stay near the fire with James. I feel like perhaps he wants to ask me to leave. I look over my back. I don't see Samantha or Sarah. They're silent in their shack. Anything could happen right now and as the possibilities run through my head my palms grow sweaty, and I start to shake. I've my handguns with me, but I have no desire to get into a gunfight. Nor will I die.

"You said you were heading to Central America, right?"

"I was." I rub my hands, trying to make sure the sweat won't slow me down in a gunfight. James stares into the fire. The flame dances its last gasp. The few blackened chips from which it rises are all that remains of the fuel for the night.

"Not anymore?"

What do I say? Do I beg? "Well... I was hoping that I could stay here for a little. I think I told you the main point of my heading down there was to find people..." I keep my head tilted down.

"And now that you found them, why keep going?"

"Well, I'm not saying that exactly. I'll leave if you want. I'm fine with that. But I'm also fine with recuperating until the winter passes. I don't think I'll get to warm country before then," I say and look up at the clear sky. There have been few nights where the night sky has broken the cloud cover.

My memory of the night that Jenny died, reminds me of this. But the memories I have of that night are not crystal clear. Nor have whatever traces of reality that my brain decided to keep, been solid. They have shifted, more than normal memories care to shift. Yet this sky, right here, right now, is an amazing piece of art. I see bright stars; I see the blur of the Milky Way.

James follows my eyes and looks up. "That's not something you see everyday," he says.

I wait for him. He's trying to pull himself to say what he needs to say.

"So you want to stay?"

"If that's all right with you."

He doesn't answer. Instead he looks at the last few flames licking the air, now a little more furious and random than before, as if the fire knows that this is its last moment here on earth and it's trying to make a case for us to feed it more fuel, to allow it a little more time on this earth.

"Do you read the Bible, Tom?"

"I have. Not well enough to know its nuances, though," I say and glance around; the shadows are growing weaker; the light is giving way to the dark. The unknown of the night. The dark where Samantha could be hiding with a gun. It wouldn't take much. I remember how I felt in that cave: alone, the piece of warmth that was an aberration to the coldness of the world that wanted to invade, defeat me. I wonder which death would be better: here with a bullet to the back of my head, or alone in the cave, surrounded by all the amenities one could want in a post-apocalyptic land. I take deep slow breaths to calm myself down. If

31

it is to be, it will be, I think. I will not kill this man, because I fear what I will do to the women.

"Well, I read it a lot. You still believe?"

"I don't know, tell you the truth. I'm not certain what to believe these days." I remember how Jenny had said that she didn't believe anymore. That it didn't seem to make sense here. Of course that was after I'd done *that* to her. Me, the monster.

"You're not?" James asks, the color of incredulousness in his voice. "You don't see God's hand in all of this? In us meeting you. In Him allowing you to live?"

I look at him. I've always been pretty religious. Not fervent, but I went to church, did the works of charity to show I believed, and really did see His hand in all that was good in the world. The person who believed that, however, had not done what I was forced to do.

James seems like the fundamentalist kind of person that I normally would have eschewed. Normally. Back then. Now, however, I see the gleam in his eyes as a beacon of hope, not something to ignore politely. "I don't know if I see His hand in this, this destruction. You do?" I ask wondering if he really can look at all this death and see our Maker in it.

"But His hand *is* in this. You remember the great flood, right? How everyone on earth forgot His name and just lived for themselves? You remember that, right?"

I nod.

"Well, this is his way of getting rid of all the sinners in the world, of testing the true believers. Don't you see?"

I nod again to buy some time. I try not to clench my jaw, or in any way give away my displeasure in his reading of the Good Book. There is nothing wrong—

scholastically speaking—with his view; it's just that I'm thinking about Jenny and that if I were to accept James' view, then I would be committing her memory to an eternal prison. Jenny didn't believe, and so she was killed. It wasn't anything I did that drove her to kill herself; instead, it was her vile soul that allowed God to watch her die. The same would go for Carol. I simply couldn't allow them to be tainted like this.

"No." I temper my voice so it's soft. "I don't see. I don't think that the people I loved died because they were sinners. They were... better than me."

"No, Tom." James reaches across with his hand and places it on my thigh. It's a touch I haven't expected, and I like it.

"They may have been good, but God works in mysterious ways. He must be testing you, your faith. And I know if you believe in Him, He will know that your heart is true. And their deaths will not have been for naught," James says.

I look into his eyes as he speaks. The power and certainty with which he speaks grips my heart. And his words are bundled with friendship. Would I dare turn it down?

But Jenny. Her smell lingers in my mind as I think on her, the warmth of her body.

"No, they wouldn't have," I say to keep James from wondering what I could be contemplating. He barely nods, his face a mural of lines and shadows, never quite defined as the flames spit out their last song.

Jenny... The Pavlovian arousal of my member reminds me of that fateful night. And the night after, when it seemed that she'd accepted me.

But she hadn't. She turned her back on me in the end. That Jenny didn't want to see me any more, starts to grind against my flesh. She hadn't believed, and that's why she threw herself into the abyss. It was an innocent mistake, and yet right now, feeling the warmth from James face, so sure about his place in life, I know that I can't go on believing that there's nothing out there. There *has* to be something to strive for.

But Jenny.

Am I going to throw her image, everything we shared, to the dustbin of history?

"Maybe you're right," I mutter.

James nods his head. "I am."

"And what are your plans with your family?"

He doesn't reply or react.

"They're your family, aren't they?"

"Yes, they are. We will wait here until God calls us."

"What about finding other humans, helping them. Starting the good work again. Isn't that what the Bible says? Go forth and multiply, isn't that in the Bible?"

He doesn't agree or disagree, not with words, not with his body. He gets up. The fire is out. All that's left are embers from the magical chips and the darkness of the night is almost upon us.

"You'll be staying with us," is all James manages to muster; he does an odd shaking movement with his head, walks to the shack and disappears from sight.

I look up. The stars beam down. This infinitesimal sight of something that is far away—yet feels so close one should be able to touch it—doesn't move me as much as it should. The stars and our relationship to them are merely a contrived thought. All I can really think about, or what I feel, is how pleased I am to have James accept me. Nothing about the stars could ever match that, could it? And yet people in the past have looked up to the stars and found some meaning, especially when they thought they were anything but burning balls of gas, exuding energy until they collapsed on themselves.

I kick the embers; a low rotting feeling has started to gnaw at my insides. I decide that it will be better to sleep, to have the breathing of James and his family beside me.

That night, as I sleep, I dream I am running, far away. I wake up, sweating, the dream slipping away. Is someone after me? Maybe. And there, in the real world, in front of me, is Sarah. She's standing over me, doing the mumbling in some tongue—is it a made up child's tongue? I'm not sure—and I look for her parents only to see that they are still sleeping. Samantha has her leg over James, her head on his shoulder. It's a familiarity that I miss. Sarah seems to have stopped her mumbling, and I feel that she isn't sleepwalking.

"Sarah," I whisper. "Is something wrong?"

She continues to mumble; it's almost soothing.

I rest my head on the clump of a jacket that I call my pillow and keep an eye on her. I feel woozy watching this ritual of hers. I must ask her parents what it is she's doing, saying.

After a few minutes of mumbling, Sarah shuffles over to her bed and lies down in it. My dream swallows me immediately after.

"Do you know what Sarah says when she mumbles?" I ask.

I'm alone with James. We've gone to look for more rocks. Sarah has now taken to fashioning them into faces of all sorts. It adds to the ambience of the shrine they have going; though I've stopped calling it a shrine

35

once Samantha reminded me it wasn't a shrine, that in fact it was only an artists' station, to allow the mind to roam free, as we were all Christians who wouldn't dare catch ourselves dead in something as heathenistic as a shrine.

"No," James says. The shake of his head is not one of a father who wishes that the mumbling would stop.

"Is it some language she learned?"

"I don't think so."

"None whatsoever?"

"No." James shakes his head as he picks up a rock.

"You sure? She might have picked up something from school, TV or the Internet."

"Oh no," James says. "We kept her away from those public schools; Sarah was home-schooled."

"Ah," I say, thinking how odd I used to think such people were. Yet it would appear that being home-schooled is something that saved them. Why dwell on something only because it used to be culturally odd—especially when that culture has destroyed itself?

"And she was never allowed on the Internet, or near a TV. No her language is unique. We're certain that God gave it to her."

I try to look like this doesn't shake me as much as it does. Yet in the end, looking at the wasteland that science left us, wouldn't it be foolish to not hang hope on God?

"God?"

James nods, picks up a rock, examines it, throws it into his bag. He looks up to the peak; we're at its base.

"Have you tried to see what it means?" I ask.

"I..." He considers this for a second. "We just want for her relationship with Jesus to bloom. You know?"

"Right," I say, though I'm really thinking that perhaps they're as frightened and confused of this new world as I am.

My heart settles. "I've a few questions, if you don't mind."

"Go ahead, Tom. You're allowed questions."

"What happened?" I wipe the air around me with my hand.

"You mean us?"

"No, the bombs."

"Oh." He pauses for a second. "I told you God was angry. I think we lost our way as a nation, as humans, and God decided to impart a lesson to us. With all the technology in the world we were told that we didn't need God." He pauses again, huffs out a half laugh. "But in the end the All-Mighty showed us just what a life without him leads to."

I want to quarrel about a few things, but I agree with his sentiment; it felt like, during those last days that things would've been better in the world if more people *did* believe in the powers of Christ. Still, this isn't what I was getting at. Bill had showed me a few newspaper clippings, but I didn't believe them anymore.

"I mean what the people did for the bombs to be launched?"

"Oh that. I'm not certain; like I said, we were out here on a geological survey when everything went down. I wasn't paying that much attention, though I should have. A bomb hit Miami... I remember that being big. Then another in some Chinese city. Cities around the world," he says, scratching his head.

"Dirt bombs?"

"I don't know. There was a lot of blaming going about. Some people were certain the Chinese were paying off people to do it. I think it went both ways, connections were found, and... God's work." He reaches out his hand and clasps my shoulder.

I cannot deny the power of his touch. It travels from my skin to my brain, organs, soothing.

"I have to ask some more questions about... Those men. Did you know them?"

"Yes, I thought I said as much?"

I have to make sure that I don't drop any clues as to what the boy had told me as he died. "I mean, you didn't seem so distraught. Nor did Sarah."

"That was." He stops mid sentence, clenches his jaw.

My insides churn, I want to take it back. James seems to be drifting away from me. "It's all right," I say, "I understand..."

"Thanks," James says; there's hesitation in his voice.

The air between us is still laced with something I cannot quite name, something that doesn't bode well for our future together, of me staying with his family. I look up at the peak. It's a smooth round dome, orange like the rest of this place. "You ever climb?"

"No." He glances at me. "You?"

"Yeah, love it." I walk over to the base and tap the rock. I haven't had a chance to examine the rock—not for this purpose. Was I strong enough to get up there? The sides of this peak climbed straight up. It wasn't going to be easy. There are several cracks, small holds. I test one. The rock's easy to grip, almost like sand paper. Of course that means that it'll scrape skin off. I've never climbed something this tall—it looks at least a thousand feet high now—without the use of rope or chalk.

James's boring a hole through the back of my head with his eyes.

"You're going to climb, it, aren't you?" he asks, the tension and excitement in his voice is palatable.

I turn. He's grinning. When I'm not probing into his family life, James's downright likeable in every way. I smile back and take off my shoes.

"Take this, and see what you can see." He hands me a small pair of binoculars. I stuff them into my pocket, making sure its strap is looped around my belt loop. I take a deep breath, look around for all the possible routes, before I jump up and grab one with my hand, my feet wedged into a crack that seems to extend up for a few hundred feet. My other hand goes into the crack. I follow it up.

I wonder if the rock will break off. I've no idea what kind of rock I'll face up there.

The crack ends, and I look around for holds. My hand catches one, but as my foot rests on one hold, it immediately gives way, and my body lurches to the ground. Luckily, my handhold is strong, and I dangle from one hand and slowly place my foot on the hold that I'd missed. My other foot finds a small hole, and I fit a toe in. I can feel my heart in my mouth, a taste much like blood on my tongue. I turn my head down, though I know I shouldn't. James is but a speck. I must be several hundred feet up. I can see that Samantha and Sarah have joined him. Sarah is waving her hands, jumping and clapping. The sounds reach me like some distant whispers that a lover might murmur in my ear. A gust of wind tugs me away from the wall. My forearms start to twitch. I'd better get a move on.

Which way though?

I look at the horizon and back down. If I slip, I will die. There is no doubt about that. I take another breath. There is nothing else to do, I remind myself. A slow need to get to the top, to not fail, comes over me. I feel stronger, my forearms quiet down, and I test holds. I traverse horizontally, then upwards. Hold after hold, like a machine, like meditation.

I pull myself over the top and lie on my back. After I catch my breath, I sit up. The wind whistles. I take out my binoculars. We're in what appears to be a basin ringed with mountains to the north and west, while less audacious hills ring the rest of the basin's circumference. Directly to the north, before the mountains, is my cave. I try to make out the entrance, but fail.

As I stretch out my forearms and contemplate the way back down—going down was always the hardest part—a glint in the southern horizon catches my eye. I look through my binoculars and try to make out what it is. What ever it is, it is too far for my binoculars to make out. A haze blurs the distance. I lie down and rest my elbows on the ground. All I can make out is something glittering... but how? There's no sun out. Perhaps over there... Then I think I see smoke, several spires billowing into the air. Or not. It could be a mirage. But I'm excited and wonder if perhaps there are other people out here.

I scan elsewhere again to make sure I didn't miss anything. I look back and forth on the basin; I see nothing.

Then I see a speck of black to the northeast. I steady my hands. It's a man, dressed in black, a backpack on his shoulders and a gun on top of that. If he continues on the trajectory he's on, he'll run into us.

I climb down, anxious to tell the family what I saw.

"Well?" asks James.

"I saw a man heading in this direction. And I think I saw signs of more people."

Samantha offers me some soup. "For your effort." She smiles.

I gobble it up.

"You think the man is dangerous?" James has his rifle.

Sarah stares at me with awe. "Can you teach me to climb like that?"

"Not now honey." James gives Samantha a look, and she takes Sarah's hand.

I watch as the two women descend to the shacks.

"He has a rifle, and he's moving here," I say.

"We could see if he just passes."

"Not sure if that's a good idea."

"Why risk a confrontation?"

"All right, but we have to watch him, and we don't want to surprise him."

"Where was he?"

I walk him to the northern side of the base. For a second I wonder if the man's already climbing up to us. If he surprises us, it wouldn't end well. I pull out my handgun, and James jumps back at the sight of it.

I shrug. Surely he knew I had some weapon on me. James pretends to dust himself off.

"There?" James points at a black speck, bigger than before, moving towards us.

I look through the binoculars. "It's him." I can make out his face now, and he doesn't appear to be particularly nice, or bad. He only looks at where he's stepping before trudging forward, as if in pain.

I hand the binos to James who takes a look. "He doesn't look friendly."

"We should stay low, so he doesn't see us," I say. We both get down on the ground.

The man edges closer and closer. He'll soon be at the base of our hill.

"What do you think? He looks like he's heading straight for us."

"I know," James replies, with his voice betraying his anxiety. "We should still hope he passes."

The sun's minutes away from the horizon. "Night will be here, James. Do you want someone nearby without knowing where he is?"

This comment seems to sink into James, though he doesn't reply. I can hear him breathing, loudly, like there are images in his head that are more frightening than what's in front of him.

"I think we should meet up with him, before it gets dark. We can go down, talk to him, from higher ground, then let him stay the night. We'll keep an eye on him, and in the morning we can send him on his way." I look at James. There has been, in the past few minutes, a shift in the power structure between us. Before James was in control. Now, danger present, it appeared that I am.

Instead of accepting my role graciously, the voice inside me growls. I think of Samantha, and even Sarah. I remember looking at Samantha when her underwear showed as she bent over. I think of taking that. There's even the thought that we can let this man into our compound, and I can let down my guard, let him take out James. Then I can take the man out... Could I be any more of an animal?

"I think you're right," James says as his voice cracks.

"I am."

I get up, help James to his feet, and we slowly make our way down. "Make sure you keep an eye on him."

"I will."

The man's at the base of our hill and close enough that we don't need the binos anymore. He pulls out a small flask and drinks. He doesn't hold the bottle to his mouth for long. I can tell from the angle that it's empty.

When we are about fifty feet away, I tell James to keep his rifle pointed on the man at all times. I walk a few feet away, making sure my handgun is loaded.

"Hello there!" I yell out.

The man spins, has his rifle in his hands in less than a second, and points it in my direction. I duck behind a rock, my head poking out to maintain a glimpse of him.

"Who is it?" the man snarls.

I peek my head over the top of the rock. He's old, gnarled on the edges. I'm not certain this will end well. My heart's in my mouth, spilling the taste of blood everywhere. "We're only here to meet with you, help you out a little."

"I don't need no body's help. Show yourself."

It's an order I don't like. I remember the bottle. "You need water, don't you? We can give you some and send you on your way."

"Show yourself," the man repeats. Spittle flies from his mouth.

I can see why he'd want to see me, but I don't feel much like becoming a target; not when his voice is this angry. And in a gunfight my handgun wouldn't match his rifle, not from this distance. "Put down the rifle first." I look over at James who, wedged between two rocks, is trying hard not to move. He appears to have a shot of the man. I don't want to lay my life at the feet of James' ability to shoot straight and quick. There's also the feeling that perhaps I should have let James go ahead.

"Why should I do that?" the man says, laughing. "So you can kill me easier?"

"No, I swear, we don't intend to harm you."

"We? Then all of you show yourselves."

"I'll show myself, but lay down your gun."

The man lets out another nasty laugh.

"All right, just don't point it here." I decide that, since we have almost hit dusk, I might as well show myself. In a short while the man will be able to run and hide in the rocks, and we'll be in a tricky situation. I stand up from behind the rock.

The man squints, lowers his rifle. "Well, and your friend?"

I hear James move and it's too late to say anything because he has already stepped up from his rock.

"Ah, there he is," the man says. "Now you lower *your* gun."

James obeys. I want to slap him.

"We're coming down," I say and start to make my way down. I take my steps carefully to make sure that I'm keeping an eye on him, and stepping over the loose rocks. My hands tremble; I feel exposed.

When we get down, I put out my hand, hoping to salvage some sense of a good feeling. "I'm Tom."

"Call me MacGee," the man says.

"James."

We all shake hands. From here I can see the man is old. He looks to be in his fifties. Perhaps older. He has a bent back, and his hands look scarred. His face is beaten by sun, and is lined with wrinkles that look like they've been etched in by charcoal. His eyes are almost gray, and he doesn't really look at us. Though his voice is rusted, he appears to be nice.

"We have a place you can stay at." I point up the hill in front of us. "James, lead the way."

James turns, and I nod at MacGee to follow behind him. I'll make sure that he's where I can see him at all times.

We make our way up the rocks and are back at the shacks just as it gets dark.

"Nice place," MacGee notes. "How long did it take you to build it?"

"Others helped," James says quickly. The rest of his family haven't shown their faces yet. I understand, as I don't want this man to see the women before we've seen what his true colors are. Yet there's something in James that's odd...

"So, MacGee, where are you from? What's your story?" I ask as I pass him a bottle of water, which he guzzles down, the tendons in his neck contract and expand. I can smell him clearly, and he smells of ammonia.

He finishes drinking as the darkness falls. James starts a fire, and the flames lick all our faces. MacGee's face seems especially made for the light of a fire. His age has melted all the fat from his face, so the sharp angles of his bones jutting out, and his wrinkles highlighted, look fearsome and dignified at the same time. I feel a slight sense of affection for him. This disappears as I catch him giving a look of death at James. Something's not right.

"Well, I was a prospector, living in the mountains about a couple days from here."

"Prospector?" I ask.

"Yep. The price of gold was sky high." He threw his hand above his head. "And I'd just had me a huge find. Whole nuggets in the side of a mountain I'd dynamited." He shook his head. "Then this mess happened. What's the price of gold now? Nothing, I tells ya. Food and water's all that matters now." He shakes his head, hacks, and spits near his feet. "Suppose it was always meant to be. Like this." He waves his hands about. We're getting too complex for what we're made. Can you imagine paying millions for a painting now?" He pulls out a flask and takes a swig. Then he hands it over to me.

I can smell the alcohol, even though it's a few feet away; my nose tickles. I reach for it and sniff. It's stout.

"Made it myself. Was the other thing that I used to do."

"Moonshine," James says, the disapproval apparent in his voice.

"That's right. MacGee's best. Give it a try. It's the one thing that still has value these days."

I can feel James boring a hole into me. He doesn't approve. But I don't care. After what happened during the past few hours, I feel that I'm in control here. I take a swig. The liquid splashes from my tongue to my throat, as clear and light as spring water, before it leaves a torching flame in its wake. My throat seizes up, and I cough.

MacGee laughs. "See? Whadda tellya? Good stuff eh?"

I smile. "Thanks. That's some rough stuff." I think that I like MacGee already.

46

"I know, I know. This is what makes it worth living just a little longer, am I right?"

James is now seething, almost comically so. "That's right," I say as the sip of alcohol settles in my stomach like a rock, and I can feel its every little molecule burst into my blood stream, and I sense the encroachment of a pliable sense of reality, a giddy reaction that I cannot help but welcome. I am close to drunk from one sip of liquor.

I smile then laugh. It's as if all my worries have been lifted, that I'm no longer in a post-apocalyptic nightmare and am in my own cocoon of thoughts; the thoughts are soft, friendly. I laugh again.

McGee laughs with me.

James stares at us like we're mad.

I don't like it.

I grab the flask from MacGee.

"Drink." I push the flask in James' face. He stares at it like it's an abomination, and I can tell he wants to give me a piece of his mind.

"No thanks."

"Oh, come on, drink." MacGee joins in with my demand. "It'll lighten your load. You're too uptight."

"I'm all right," James says, as he clenches his jaw.

"Don't be so weak all the time. A little drink never hurt anyone," I say and step up to him, pushing the flask hard into his chest. James flinches for a second and I know that I've won.

He lifts the bottle to his mouth and takes a swig. The proceeding choke and spit of liquid has me and MacGee laughing. James sits down.

I sit down as well. I know that I haven't drank that much in a while, and I've lost a lot of body weight, but I'm certain that MacGee's added something extra to the liquor. I look over at James, perhaps he was right for not wanting to drink, perhaps drinking from a stranger would be foolish. I want to scold myself, but I hold back. After all, MacGee also drank from the same bottle. So how could it be poisoned?

James smirks. "It is good," he says.

I grin back as my mind whirrs. It's then that I hear a rock smack in to other rocks. Possibly a rockslide. I hear it again. I'm used to silent nights. In fact, I'm certain that that wasn't the wind making a sound. Is MacGee not alone? "I gotta piss," I say and stand up. I walk away from the small flame, making sure that I'm in the darkness.

I notice MacGee staring James down. They start a conversation, but it feels forced. Is he trying to hide something? I think about what we saw. It's quite possible that MacGee has someone else with him.

Where? We didn't see anyone with him. I feel myself getting woozy. I touch my handgun; it's still there. I'm a little angry that I let my guard down so quickly.

Taking the stairs out of the compound area, I walk to where I first pointed out MacGee's figure to James. It's too dark to see anything. The cloud cover is back, and I can't even make out the outline of the peak next to me. I wait for my eyes to adjust. Behind me I can hear MacGee and James chatting. It sounds more natural now, but I'm still not convinced that everything is all right. I pull out my cock and start pissing, darting my head back and forth. I hear nothing. I zip back up and take in deep breath.

Another rock slides. I tense up; my skin shrivels; there has to be someone or something out there. I walk carefully to where I heard the sound. I can hear it now, a more consistent buzzing, mixed with a loud secreting noise. Now I can hear it. It is reacting to me, this noise, this horrible noise, that sounds like it will, just by virtue of the vibrations it's making, tear apart the fibers of my muscles and eat me whole. I pull out my flash light, slip on the red lens, to cover what I'm doing, and flash it in the direction of the sound.

What meets my eyes is a group of what could only be called insects. They're black, the size of my thumb with multiple thick antennas that flicker in the direction they move. They're coming from underneath the ground; there're so many that they push the rocks to surface. And I realize that they're not feeling, but eating, and they are ingesting a small packet of open food, which Sarah had earlier. The food is soon gone, and I watch as the insects disappear into the ground.

I walk quickly back to the fire. I feel things crawling all over my skin. I know that it's only my mind playing tricks on me.

"Well, that was a long piss," MacGee says, giving me a suspicious eye.

"Yeah," I say, trying to present a face that is composed, not scared. I don't want to lose the power I gained, not over James at least. I realize that I forgot all about MacGee's possible partner. I point to the flask. "You put something else besides alcohol in that?"

"You mean poison?" MacGee says, a little too defensively for my tastes.

"No, I mean something good." I try to smile as if I'm all about taking the drugs, but I don't think it comes across as believable because MacGee's face is still in a half-snarl.

"Well there ain't nuttin' in there but alcohol."

James, who appears to have relaxed a little, gives me a look as if to ask why I'm being so confrontational. I sit down.

"I saw some insects up there. Never seen them before." I stop there because I want to see what they have to say before I go on.

"You mean ants?" James asks; he's sitting straight, not looking so out of it anymore.

"No, I've seen the ants before."

"I've seen them on the bodies, afterwards."

"So have I," I reply then wonder if I have told James that I've seen any dead bodies yet. "I mean something else."

"What they look like?" MacGee asks.

"Black." I hold out my forefinger and thumb in a circle. "About this big. They'd little, I don't know, pincers."

"From the ground, right?"

"Right, from the ground. They were moving rocks there were so many." As I speak I can see the eyes of the two men on me, glued with an intensity that I enjoy.

"What were they doing?" James asks.

"Eating a piece of food that Sarah left."

"Damn," MacGee says.

"Well, I think it settles what's been eating up the bodies, right?" asks James.

MacGee shrugged. "Haven't seen bodies, myself."

I wonder if he's bullshitting us, trying to maintain some sort of higher moral ground, or is he serious about not seeing anything die out here? Why was he so wary of us at first? I hold off on challenging him.

"Yeah, that makes sense," James says. "The ants were too small to eat that much flesh that quickly."

"Good news is that they left the wrapper alone."

"They eat dead bodies?" MacGee says.

I look him over; he's staring at his flask

"Yeah, they eat dead bodies," I reply. "What I'm worried about, and tell me if this is far fetched, is what if they don't get enough dead bodies. Then what? They'll come after us? And if not us, what about our food?"

"You said the wrapper was left alone, right?" James asks.

"Yeah, but how much hunger would it take for them to bite through that?"

James looks at MacGee's flask. MacGee glances back at him, strokes his jaw, and grins.

"You thinking the same thing as me, ain't ya?" MacGee says and lets out a laugh. "Go ahead." He pushes the flask to James.

This time James isn't hesitant, and he puts the bottle to his mouth, though I'm certain he doesn't drink.

"I think if they leave the wrappers alone we'll be fine. Some things just don't go getting a taste for live humans," James says.

"Really? You think that once they have no more food they'll even worry about the semantics of a live or dead human?" And as I say this I get the chills, a creeping sensation, to which I brush my neck, but feel nothing.

"Well, there's not much we can do. No use frettin' over it. Just keep moving on, that's what I say," MacGee says and reaches out for his flask. James hands it over to him, and MacGee takes a drink from it. He looks at me, and I shake my head. No need for any more drink than I have right now.

"You have more, right?"

MacGee shakes his head as if it's a silly question.

"You know how to make more. Right?"

"Yeah, it'll be hard to get the ingredients, though."

"What's needed?"

"Barley works best, but I suppose any grain would do."

I think about the supplies in the cave.

"How can you talk about alcohol, when there's still the matter of the insects?" James says, and I don't like the return of some sort of power in his voice.

"Not much we can do about the insects," MacGee says. "Unless you have insecticide on ya."

"I don't. But we can plan," James says.

This doesn't sound like the man who always trusted in God. "The insects haven't come for us yet, or torn into our food supplies," I say.

"Science? Let's not bring that into the equation," James says.

I immediately see the reaction on MacGee's face, and it's not friendly. "What's wrong with science?" he says while crunching up his face at James, then looking at me, as if for support.

"It's what got us into this mess to begin with, so I think I'm safe in saying we should stay away from it. Let's not forget God."

"Whaddaya mean science got us into this mess? Seems to me that people got us into this were people. Nothing more. Science. God. Same result," MacGee says.

"How can you say that?" James is now squaring up to MacGee.

I'll be forced to take sides, and though I have an attachment to James and his family, I like MacGee too. His words are not without wisdom.

"Easy you two. The last thing we need is a war over a minor matter. Let's get back to the insects." As I say the word "insects" I feel how the two men stop staring at each other.

"Daddy?" Sarah comes running out of the shack, Samantha runs behind her, as if she's catching her, and she does, and picks her up.

"Sorry," Samantha says.

"Daddy, what were you fighting about?"

I sheepishly smile at Samantha, who gives me a fierce look.

"Nothing honey." James steps over the fire and lifts Sarah into his arms. "We were just discussing some issues. Nothing to worry about."

"And what are these insects?"

I smirk.

MacGee's face has lightened up; I even think that I see his wrinkles disappear. He now has the look of a grandfather as he looks at Sarah. He tips his head at Samantha. "Good to meet you miss, the name's MacGee," he says but doesn't put out his hand. "And you?" he tips his head at Sarah, who is regarding him rather coolly.

"I'm Sarah." She puts out her hand, and he gets up and makes a show of kissing it.

"So you must be the princess."

Sarah turns suddenly shy and buries her head into her father's shoulder.

"She's shy," Samantha says as she walks over. "But she'll warm up to you soon. I'm Samantha."

"Well pleased to meet you." MacGee goes through the same show of kissing her hand, and Samantha blushes. In his antics, there's no leering, nothing of what I've done.

Even James seems to take MacGee's quickly cemented relationship with his two women well. I feel like an outsider.

"Well, I'm sure that she's a fine young lady," MacGee says. He doesn't appear slighted, or surprised that I and James kept the women from him.

My attention shifts to the darkness. I don't feel the chill or the creepiness that I did only moments ago. Even though the scene between MacGee and James' family is unfolding without me, I feel the camaraderie pulsing from them and into me. And I feel more human than I have since Jenny's death—since the fall. My jealousy of MacGee dissapates, even as I see Sarah get down from her father's arms and start to ask questions about his flask. There is nothing out there, but there is us. And that feels all the more a powerful drug. The flames have now brightened up as James throws a few more chips in.

"Well, Tom here." MacGee points to me as he speaks. "He believes that there's more than just alcohol here." He summons me over with his hand, and I step closer.

He's doing this on purpose, pulling me into the conversation, and I am thankful for that.

"Tom climbed the mountain," Sarah says, and when James and Samantha give me a look of awe, as does Sarah, I feel vindicated, almost foolishly so, for everything I had done until that moment.

"I did," I say, and I remember the smoke spirals. And if the moment between me and these four people had been a brief second for me to feel like I wasn't in a drab world, with deadly insects, and if for that brief moment I was full of hope, it was all dashed as I recall the smoke spirals. There're people out there, and possibly lots of them. Even though MacGee and this family have turned out to be friendly, my experiences with Bill, Big Lee, myself, tighten my brain as I think on the possible outcomes.

My pause, and obvious cogitation must have caught MacGee's eye because he gives me a look. "Something wrong," he says more than asks.

"I..." I say and by now the thought of meeting up with people and the confrontation it involves has tightened the rest of my body, as if it's preparing for impact of the ground. I know the evil that confrontation brings out in me.

"Tom," MacGee says, loudly now, as he has a worried look on his face. "Is it the insects getting to you?"

"No," I say. "There were several, or lots, of smoke coming from the southern direction."

"A fire?"

"No. Smoke rising up. Multiple fires... People," I say, the words coming out of my mouth like they're meant to be barbs, and it works, on Sarah at least, as she buries her head in MacGee's lap.

"Just a fire has you spooked?" James says, his face almost a sneer.

I know I've lost some of my stature, but I feel like I don't care.

"What if someone saw *our* fire?" James says.

"This fire," I say the word fire as angrily as I can summon. "Is not a fire. It's small. It doesn't smoke. No one more than a few hundred meters away will be able to see it."

"Now hold on just a second." MacGee puts out his hand to steady the tension. It works. I wonder how someone like him could ever be a lonely man in the mountains.

"I saw a huge fire out this ways. That's why I started moving in the first place," MacGee says.

"Was it a huge billowing black cloud? With some explosions too?" asks James.

I hold my breath. That could only have been my fire.

"Yep, I think I heard explosions, but as far away as I was, there was no way to tell," says MacGee. "I was hoping it was a signal, but if it wasn't you." MacGee looks at James who shakes his head. "Then who did it and why?"

I nod my head slightly as I feel their eyes darting towards me, then away. The longer I wait the more suspicious my silence becomes. Tension creeps back into my blood. The night closes in on me. I think, for a moment, that the fire in front of us is dying out, but it rushes back to life, lighting the people around it, and I notice that in fact they're looking at me. And James is staring at me the hardest.

"It came from your direction, didn't it?" James asks me.

"It was me," I say, my voice calm. "I found an abandoned shipping container; it was contaminated. Or so I think, and I decided to burn it. To bring people to it as well." I point to MacGee. "So it worked to some level." I hope that they don't dig too deep.

I'd lied to Jenny, and coming here, I hoped to forget her and what I did to her. Now, like bits and pieces, the real I is coming back into focus, and I am the same. I fend off that thought, try to make my brain follow other ghosts. I remind myself that it's not really a lie because they'll never find out about what I've done, not if I don't want to tell them. And if they don't know—after all, are they going to go digging for the bodies?—and I suppress these thoughts, then isn't it all as if it never happened?

"Now why did you go and burn a perfectly good shipping container?" MacGee asks, breaking my train of thought. "What kind of contaminate?"

I look at MacGee. "I don't know, radiation, I think."

The old man laughs. "Well, better get to burning the world all over again."

My heart starts beating fast. Once I see them as people who don't trust me, how can I trust them? "It was needed, worse than anywhere else," I say with a forcefulness that I hope they take for hurt defensiveness, and instead of my true feelings, or the truth. "And it worked as far as bringing you here." I point to MacGee.

"It did," MacGee says with a slight shrug, and he looks at the fire.

The family follows suit and I feel good for a second. But my mind won't rest. It's looking for an enemy, and I see how quickly the family follows MacGee's body language and for a second my mind says: they're tricking you, how can they speak to each other that well without having known each other for longer than the few minutes you have seen here? That doesn't just happen. They knew each other before.

They're trying to trick you.

I beat that voice down; I try and strangle it because I know where it will lead. I try to think of something to say before the emptiness of the night swallows me, makes me realize that I'm alone and that listening to these voices in my head is fine because they are looking for a way to survive, and in this world with no other law it is fine to just survive.

"But that other fire is different. I don't think it's a signal; I just think it's people. I mean... I can't imagine another reason for a fire, can you?"

The thoughts that seems to pass over everyone's mind, telegraphed through their faces, seem to be ones that are taking my words into consideration. I keep down a smile. I am free. As long as we have something else to work towards, I am free.

"I agree," MacGee says after a short pause. "It sounds very plausible."

The fire is flickering, the last few gasps for air, and in that second, as James picks out a few more chips to throw on, and I wait for the family to agree with what MacGee has said, I feel like the loneliest person in the world. What use was it to find these people if there was just going to be animosity between us? That moment where I felt a connection with James, with a God up above is gone, and I wonder why this is. Is something wrong with me? Was the loss of Carol, then Jenny, still weighing on my mind?

I don't want to continue the conversation, but James throws the chips on the fire and the flames greedily swallow it up. It's as if they're beings that will never be satisfied with the way things are, will always ask for more and will take what you give and burrow a hole into your soul. I know this last part seems far-fetched, but since the fire, and the accompanying light, and the fact that I have to, or will have to stay up and talk to these people, these veritable strangers, tears into me, I can't help but believe it.

"Shouldn't we spare the chips?" I ask.

No one answers me, each in their own bubble. MacGee takes me in; he seems to have registered my silent cogitation and sudden outburst in a knowing nod. Though I'm normally annoyed by such actions, in an old man like MacGee I feel that it's fatherly, and I like it, accept it.

"If it concerns you that much I'll go with you and check it out," MacGee says and breaks the silence, and for a second I wonder what he's talking about. My look must have registered because he continues: "With the smokes. We can go and check 'em out. That way we can see if there's a threat. You know?"

I nod, though I'm not that sure that I want to see more people.

"I'm not sure about that," James says.

I feel grateful. But I don't want to say thank you, or even agree.

"Why not?" MacGee says, and again I sense the tension from their previous disagreement and soak my worries in that.

"I was just saying," James says.

"Nevermind. We won't. Not for now. We just have to figure out things such as food and the insects. Then we'll check out the fires. All right?"

James nods, while MacGee takes me in, and after a few seconds nods.

I catch Samantha looking at me. I see the bulge of her hips and I feel a growth in my chest. No fighting. Not now.

"I have a cave full of food that we should transfer here. That way we can keep an eye on it and make sure that the insects don't get it. After all, we don't have much in the way of food supplies, do we?"

They all agree in murmurs.

And the last of the chips flickers out, and they all retire to the shack. I watch their figures as they disappear one by one into the mouth of the abode. I look up. I see a satellite making its way across the sky. The sign of our previous world lights me up with hope. I wonder what its function was. Perhaps it's still shooting back signals, of the photos it was taking, to some now defunct station. Perhaps it was an arm of an intelligence apparatus we had in our country, something that was supposed to keep us safe, and yet, in the end, did nothing at all. That thought scares me.

Not the lack of safety, or appearance of safety, but to think that the automated machines we made are still functioning without us. As if we're useless receptors to begin with.

I walk quickly inside. I'm thinking of philosophy classes in college, and though I am certain that having been an engineer or doctor would help the most in this new world—especially when building towards that new future—I can't help but be angry at myself for not studying philosophy since it seems so pertinent to the vacuum that I feel inside me. The one that's growling, might soon be screaming, but has already let me know that it won't be satisfied with just material goods. I let my eyes adjust to the darker stomach of the shack and wonder if the hole inside me will only be satisfied with flesh.

James points out my bed. He has placed me between MacGee and his family. For some reason he has placed Samantha and Sarah between him and me. I assume he's scared of MacGee and wants the most distance between them. I want to jump with joy at my luck. I cannot see if it's Sarah or Samantha who's closest to me. I lie down and stare up. I can hear MacGee already snoring in blissful sleep. I think I can hear James breathing deeply. I wonder if Samantha can feel my heart beating. And as my mind starts to explore the recesses of her body, those curves, I wonder what to do.

Reach over?

That look had to be for something, right? So many years and so many women, and I still feel the same rush as when I moved in to kiss my first girl.

I lift my hand slowly and wonder if anyone can hear me rustle. I will Samantha to perceive it. I will Sarah to be fast asleep. I feel someone rustle, then hear it. My heart's in my throat. Just a touch, all I want's a touch. My hand swivels over and hovers there for a second; I wonder if James knows what I'm doing, but he is drawing punctuated heaves of air that could only mean he's sleeping. I'm sure that MacGee's asleep too. I sense the cold air around me, the nights are getting chillier, but I don't feel cold, in fact I'm burning up.

Take it.

I lower my hand, and before it comes to the point where it should touch the blankets, it touches a hand.

A hand!

I caress the hand, and I'm certain that it's the larger hand that belongs to Samantha. Or am I? I feel the hand stroke mine, then pull me down. I can hear her gulp in air. It sounds like a rock dropped into a pool. It is loud. She presses my hand on her thigh.

Take it.

I try to move it, but she clasps down on my hand. Should I go for more? I decide not to. Even this, a mere thigh, is sending shockwaves through my arm and to my head. My heart feels too big for its place in my chest cavity. I'm doing something I had told myself I wouldn't do. Should I push my luck? No, I won't. I'm happy with this, because I understand what it means for her to even allow me this little touch.

And we lie there and talk like this, small taps and strokes on each other's hand and her thigh. Like some ancient language, something that perhaps our ancestors used to communicate with each other. That I've never done this before surprises me. It fills my head and heart with pure joy. I let her touch come over me; I let her speak to me and let me know how she feels. Tap, stroke. MacGee snores.

Does she love me? The swirl of questions and touches spike the pressure inside me. It's as if I'm high, the world's not as I've ever seen it before. After what seems to be hours, I pull my hand back in and drift to sleep.

The next morning I wake up to see that everyone is already up and rustling about. I look over at MacGee lying in bed, who gives me a grin and nod. It's the kind of signal that says he knows what happened. I look at him again to make sure and it's gone. Did he listen to what I did last night? Surely he couldn't have? I give him a half smile trying to tease out something, but his face doesn't reveal anything except for wrinkles.

Am I imagining things? I try to wish last night away. It was trouble to start sniffing out Samantha. Hell, I'm not completely certain that it was in fact Samantha. I watch as the family walks outside together. It feels especially cold today, and I put on an extra jacket.

MacGee's slow to get up. Even more so than a man of his age. Or the age I assume him to be. In fact he's so slow to get up, limbering himself up with the stretches of a runner, that I want to know what happened to him. What sort of life has he lived? He bends over to stretch his back, and Samantha walks in.

If I was trying to wish away the previous night, or if I wondered whose thigh I had touched for so long, her look leaves no doubt. She smiles and her eyes are so full of hope for another potential touch that I simply freeze. She walks by me and picks up something from her bed. As she does so, her hand touches my groin, and she stares into my eyes.

Blood rushes to my penis; like a fist it pushes out from my pants, hungry. I think Jenny, Carol, but only after I think I want to tear Samantha's clothes off. She's out in a flash and a: "Breakfast is ready gentlemen."

MacGee is still bent over, and I wonder if he heard something, or at least felt something. He straightens up, as I put on a hat for my head.

"It's only going to get colder, isn't it," says MacGee more so than asks.

I *really* like MacGee. I'm trying to think if he reminds me of anyone; after all that's the biggest reason to like some one, but he doesn't. He is whole and unique to himself. I can smell the food wafting in from outside. It's the set of military rations that emulates omelets and hash browns. I hear Sarah whine and her parents tersely shut her down. They are too far for me to make out the words, so I assume I have a chance to talk to MacGee.

"Well, on the part of the hemisphere that we're on, it tends to get colder at certain times of the year. Broken axis, from what I've read."

He breaks out into a smile. I'm grateful for that. I tried a sarcastic joke with James once, and it didn't work. All I got was uncomfortable silence as James took it the wrong way. Finding a person who likes your jokes, I suddenly realize, may be more important than whether or not the insects eat us alive.

"How old are you MacGee?"

He looks me over. The look tells me more than an answer. He is sensitive about his age. That only makes me want to ask him more questions.

"Why do you ask?" he growls.

"Don't know. I would say sixty from the physical appearance. Mainly I think you've been through a lot, so that might not give me a correct answer. And mainly, I want to know what it is you've been through."

MacGee glares at me. It borders on hostile, though it could also be he wants to see what I'm made of.

"Well time will allow that. We have nothing but time, don't we?" he says.

"We do."

"You, though." He points his finger at me as he says this. "Might be the kind of man who likes to chew on the time he has left." And as he says this there is a brief light of recognition and camaraderie his eyes. As if he had a brother like me, or he himself was once like me. "You might be too bold for your own good. Learn to temper that."

"What do you mean?"

He tilts his head with a smile. "Though you may be smart enough to earn yourself some extra time. And." He raises his hands to his chest, palms out, and twists his mouth to indicate he doesn't blame me. "Like I said it *is* getting cold. No one can blame you. Not least me."

I am jolted out of our moment by another call from Samantha.

"Go to her." He sticks out his hand as if ceding the way. I shake my head, hoping that my face doesn't turn completely red as I feel my face burning up.

"Fifty," MacGee says as I am about to step out.

"What?"

"Fifty. That's my age. Good guess."

"Okay," I say, though for some reason it's taking me longer than normal to register this.

"You?"

"Thirty five."

"I figured."

"You been through some tough times?"

"Me?" MacGee says with a mock-innocent face.

"Yeah. You move pretty slow, like you've broken bones."

"I have."

"From what?"

"Falls. Shots. Bombs."

"War?"

"Yep."

"Military?"

"That's usually the case. I don't go starting them on my own accord."

"Not even for a woman?"

MacGee laughs, like a hyena with a smoking habit. "That's your field bud."

I smile, but the word "bud" ignites a memory of Bill. I push it away. It feels like if I do that it'll stop bothering me. I'm not so lucky and for a second I get the image, or not the image but the exact feeling that came over me when I saw Bill's eyes before I shot him. The look was of surprise, but also something in me knew at that moment that there was a chance that Bill let me live. And if so I still killed him. *That* thought clobbers me in the balls, and I try to think of something else.

"And from the looks of it," MacGee says, and waves his hand in front of my face, "you've been through a little war of your own."

"What do you mean," but as soon as I say it I know it comes out as too defensive and MacGee smiles.

"I've seen that look before," says MacGee.

I hope he isn't right. If he is then it means that my face is more of a glass to my feelings than I thought, that I should be careful of what I even think. I make a note to try and not be so obvious next time. I can't let these people know about what it is I've done.

"Which war?" I ask, hoping the switch of subjects isn't too abrupt.

MacGee gives a half smile as if he's letting me know what he's doing, but he will allow it. "Everywhere. Really."

"And what got you into prospecting?"

"Just couldn't stand living around too many people."

"You? That doesn't seem right. You act like the kind of person who could have others eating out of his hand."

He looks down at his hands, a sad aura wafts off him. "Suppose I always did, but I know people. And that's why I couldn't stand them in the end. This..." He sweeps his hand to the surrounding area. "Is a result of people."

It still doesn't match with what I see in front of me, in this old charming man, but I decide to let it be. There'll be time for more questions later.

We eat breakfast, and I mention the food in the cave. We agree that we should move as one, and soon. After all, the longer we wait, the worse the weather will get. Samantha, out here in the open, is cold and hardly looks my way, yet there is nothing in her that hints at her avoiding me. She is an expert, and I now think that Sarah doesn't look very much like James at all.

With my sled and a couple of makeshift ones, we make our way back down. I'm up front with MacGee, while the family trudges behind us. It's slow going since we have to wait on Sarah, who, after a few hours, breaks down.

"Sarah, come on," Samantha says, cooing.

"I can't go on," Sarah whines.

I turn around when MacGee does, the family well behind us. I wonder if we should leave them behind, but decide against it.

"How long you know them?"

"I met them a week before you came around," I reply.

"Crazy world, ain't it?"

"I suppose," I say. Looking at the family, Sarah who has decided to sit on the ground, and her parents standing around her, I wonder what the chances were of finding them.

"You find them looking for something?"

"Was heading to Central America," I say, though as I spit out the words, I'm sure it's the idea of a foolish man who was desperate, one who was trying to run away from the ghosts he'd planted all around him.

"You're getting that look again."

"Oh," I say, almost wanting to crawl into a hole, while simultaneously wanting to punch MacGee— what kind of fighter would he make?

"All the way to Central America, eh?"

"That's right, not the best of ideas."

"Still. Takes a lot of balls for a man to say and do something like that. Let us just hope that you've more brains than balls."

Who is the "us" he mentioned? I let it go. "There was nothing else. I had nobody, so I assumed that the only place in the world that wouldn't be bombed would be the countries that minded their own business, the ones that were too poor for anyone to bother blowing up."

"That's magical. You were hoping for some fairness in the world?" MacGee asks, as if he's disappointed in me.

"Don't think it's a matter of fairness, just that it made sense."

"You think this world is all about not harming those who have done nothing to deserve it? You don't read much, do you?"

I don't like his insinuation. "I read. I understand the world is not fair, but I figured that with bigger fish to fry elsewhere no one would bomb Honduras."

"You figured wrong. The whole reason we had a stockpile of ten thousand nuclear bombs wasn't so we could blanket Russia, or get past whatever futile missile defense system they had, but to make sure that they had no place that they could possibly hide and survive. That was the whole idea." He shakes his head. "Bastards, the whole lot of them."

I don't reply. Not that there's much to say. He may be right; I have no way of knowing. Yet his words taste of a sort of bitterness that I don't particularly like. It doesn't inspire hope in me. It almost reminds me of the attitude Jenny held. I let the wind squeeze between us, the smell of Samantha, surprisingly, reaches me, and I look around at the area with a sense of ownership. I realize that we're near the hills on which I last made love to Jenny. It was the time before she saw me kill, before she herself had to kill, and when I thought we were the perfect couple.

"It was those religious people who started it. And they finished us all. They left us this, their grand vision of God," MacGee says suddenly and with such vehemence that it scares me. "And him." He juts his finger at James' figure, which is pulling Sarah along and perilously close to being able to hear us. "He's another one of them. We need to keep an eye on him."

The we includes me, and doesn't include the family, and though that would have made me happy last night, it worries me now. I wonder if MacGee isn't the person I should be looking to be rid off.

"What do you mean?"

"I'm saying the people who got us into this mess were a bunch of religious types like him. The generals who were calling for war, for a strike, were all a bunch of religious nuts who were secretly hoping for Armageddon because that's what they think that stupid book of theirs says."

I stop for a second, anger rising up, real anger that I haven't experienced in a while. I try to keep it down. "You're telling me you don't believe in a God?"

MacGee looks me over. The family is almost upon us. "You do? Even after all this? You watched as the bombs came down, lit up the world, the religious folks going crazy, but secretly everyone of them happy that this was one step closer to their God, and you come away from all that believing?"

"There is a God. This is his test."

MacGee lets out his car start of a laugh, laden with disrespect. The family, James especially, looks at us like they want in on the conversation, but I decide not to bring it up. I may be angry with MacGee, but I can also see using this as something to use against James in the future, especially since I've now stolen a glance at Samantha's thighs, stretching out the jean pants she's wearing.

"Sarah, you all right honey?" MacGee asks as the family comes upon us.

His charm doesn't work on Sarah whose eyes are red from crying. "No," she says.

"She tired," MacGee asks Samantha.

"Yes, she's walked a long way," Samantha says.

I hear the grace of anger in her voice, and I decide that this is an in, a way to please *her*. My balls growl.

"Sarah you want to ride on my sled?" I ask.

I see Sarah and Samantha light up, while at the same time James glares at me. Sarah lifts her arms towards me, and I pick her up and swing her on my shoulders. I decide she's light enough to carry, rather than drag. Samantha gives me a smile.

"Sarah," James says with such vehemence that I expect him to grab his daughter and pull her off my shoulders. "You're thirteen years old. Sooner or later you're going to have to act like your age."

I suppress a smile as MacGee and Samantha simultaneously admonish him.

We trudge on.

That night we sleep set up out in the open. I decide to keep away from Samantha because my penis swells at merely the thought of touching her, and I am not certain if I'll be able to control myself.

I make an excuse that I should search the nearby area for anything suspicious, and I give MacGee a look. He nods and says he'll come with me. The family hardly pays us any attention, though I see Sarah look at me like she wants to come with. There is tension between James and Samantha and I suddenly feel, and I half hope that it was and wasn't me. As we leave, they snap at each other.

We walk a ways before MacGee even speaks, which is fine by me since the sky is acting funny again. It appears as if the clouds are getting lower and lower. I wonder if it will ever rain. And if it does, will it be some sort of radioactive slush?

"Looks damn ominous, doesn't it?" MacGee says, he's noticed that I was looking up.

"I know. Almost looks like rain."

"Rain? That's impossible."

He says it with such authority.

"How do you know?"

"Hasn't rained yet. And most likely all the explosions fucked things up enough to make sure it might not rain for a long, long time."

"Why do you say that?" I remember browsing through a couple of the manuals that I took from Bill, they were very confident that rain would be constant and that it would provide, once it washed itself clean of radiation, and it had referenced some scientific sounding journals. "A manual I read said otherwise."

"Oh really?" MacGee's disgust is apparent in his tone. I wait for him to finish. "Well I guess that settles it. Tell me, where was this manual from?"

"Don't know, looked like it was put together..." I pause to remember the name of the author. It doesn't matter as MacGee cuts me off.

"By some survivalist nut? Is that what you're saying? Christ Tom, I thought you were smarter than that."

I don't like what he's said; it reminds me of the sharp words teachers in school gave me. "Who are you to say they don't have a valid point?"

"Have you seen rain yet?" he asks sharply, even partially squaring himself up to me, though he seems to immediately think better of it. "Listen. What are these people basing their observations on? Comic books?"

"I don't know."

"That's right. None of us know. The people who did know were in the government, scientists who studied poor soldiers in the Army who were made to sit through those goddamn tests of theirs. That's it. And they were studied and they saw what the consequences were... and you know what they found?" he asks as he looks at me.

"What's that?"

"We don't know. The government most likely found it to be such a hopeless situation that they classified all the information so that the masses wouldn't be furious with the fact that we held our destiny in our hands. Those stockpiles of nuclear weapons were not guarantees of safety, but the certainty of our demise. They couldn't let people know that. So they kept it silent. We can try to survive, but most likely, this is all statistical folly."

He has used some big words, but I still don't want to believe him. He sounds like a mix between a know-it-all and one of those gold bugs from when before the world was torn apart.

"Well if the government knew so much, why didn't they take precautions? I mean they must have known that there was no hope. Maybe they built shelters?"

"Doubtful. Look the government wasn't some singular entity. In the end there are people like James, those generals I talked to you about, who wanted to see the end of the world, as if it would bring their savior about."

"How can you not believe in God?" I blurt out. "I mean, what keeps you going?"

"Being human."

I scoff. I don't like that he has mentioned Christianity as the incubator of what is evil. Didn't he know that anyone with Christ in his heart can do no evil? I decide not to say this, however, and go for a slight: "So you're an animal who just survives. Is that it?"

MacGee laughs at this, and that infuriates me even more. "I'm right, aren't I?" I say.

"And what do you live for? The chance to thank Christ for what he's done for us? For testing us? Jesus, what luck," MacGee says, whispering the last part to himself.

I hold my breath. I want to defend my beliefs, but I don't want to cause too much of a rift between us. Still, I'm partially trying to convince him since I am certain that it was no belief that caused Jenny to throw herself off that cliff. "I just think a belief can help you, even in this situation."

"You hear the news as it was happening? You hear who was calling for the nuclear strike, right? It was the Christians. You remember that, right?"

"I don't," I say, though it doesn't seem right that Christians would ever say such a thing. It sounds like something a biased person would say, and even if they're right, that they chose such a violent course showed that they weren't Christians, or religious at all.

"What do you mean?"

I realize that perhaps I haven't told MacGee my cave story. I go ahead and tell him.

He doesn't laugh, just shakes his head. "So you were sheltered from it all, eh?"

"I guess."

"Lucky bastard," he says as he climbs up on a rock.

We start to climb up the slight incline of a foothill. I look back and can barely make out the figures of the family. James seems separate from the two women. "What do you mean?" I ask.

"I mean you were sheltered from it all. So you got none of the initial radiation fallout. All of us who were behind minimal shelter," he says and gestures at himself and the family. "We weren't so lucky. In fact from what I've read it means that you'll live to be older than the rest of us."

I pause to take this in. Perhaps I have been healthier, quicker than people I've met. Is that why I managed to get the jump on everyone? That some pacifist guy was allowed to mow down so many larger and more violent men? So me carrying Sarah this long was something only I could've done. "Well," I say, grateful that MacGee pointed this out. "The Lord works in mysterious ways."

MacGee laughs. "I guess he does. Or he's simply luck veiled with the mask of God by some ignorant tribesmen who didn't know that what the fuck probability was."

I don't understand his words, but I think he's trying to cut down God again. I leave it be. I can *feel* that I was chosen. "I was picked for a reason; I know it."

MacGee looks me over. "Maybe you were."

I don't know if he's mocking me or finally conceding a point. I've the feeling that I might never know which one is his true intention. "Maybe I was."

"Well, take it for what it's worth then. You'll be better off then. Especially in this new world."

I have the feeling that MacGee is not really concerned with whether or not I follow his illogical arguments. Perhaps his brain was fiddled with by radiation. "Meaning?"

"Meaning, since the people in the previous world most prepared for a nuclear war, and positioned far enough away from cities, were mostly nutty

Christians, then perhaps it's a good thing that you're one. You'll find lots of friends."

I chew on his words for a second as they seem to more than what he said

Have I found a friend in James? I don't feel that I have. There was a moment when I felt a connection, but that, I see now, was more the hand of God than anything. And yet with MacGee, I may want to throttle him, but there's something that draws me to him.

"But remember," MacGee continues. "They aren't the garden type of Christian. They're the wilder ones, and now that they've been reinforced with this nuclear war, they'll be more illogical than before.

"Remember I'm one of them too," I say, hoping that he doesn't consider me illogical.

MacGee continues to climb then stops. "I think we've seen enough. Let's head back."

The walk back is doused in complete silence.

When we get back, dusk is upon us. The low clouds must have cut off the sun's rays because there's no spectacular show of color. We all lie down in a circle with our heads pointed inward. I'm glad it doesn't afford me a chance to touch Samantha.

I promise myself that I'll control myself. Think of Jesus. Think of the commandments. I once believed, but was one of those people who thought that if you read too much, went to church too much, you'd become an extremist. Never wanted that; only thought that people with Jesus in their hearts were better people in general. I can hear MacGee already snoring, and I decide that I'll engage him in a proper debate. Perhaps not in front of the family, but sooner or later I will. I shouldn't feel like just because he's smarter that I won't stand a chance with my footing. I remember the story about the man who built his house on rock. I gain strength from this and relax.

I look at the stars. They comfort me, even though no cloud cover means we're colder. I feel closer to God, to the world he made for us. I can hear everyone breathing hard now, and I'm slowly falling asleep, the ether world of my dreams slowly luring me to close my eyes. The satellites fly by above and beam information to stations that no longer exist. It reminds me of a riddle I can't quite remember.

As my dream envelops me, I think about the people around me. It feels much better than living alone, feeling the emptiness seep into your pores and suck the life right out of you.

The next afternoon we make it to the cave. I walk in and the sight of the food hits me, then the black mass does too. I jump back out of the cave. The others, waiting for me outside, stare at me.

"What is it?" MacGee asks.

I take a second to think as well as slow my blood down. Did the insects eat the entire stock? What the hell do we fight them off with? Should I go in with a fire?

"Hey." MacGee taps me. "What is it?"

"Insects. All over the place."

"Well, let's have a look." MacGee takes out his flashlight and peers in. "I don't see anything."

I poke my head back in. The insects are gone. Scared of us. But how long before they realize that we aren't much to be frightened of? "I swear they were here just a second ago."

"I believe you," MacGee says giving me a look that tells me he's worried about me.

Will this lower my bravery stature in James' eyes? There's no trace of the insects, and they haven't damaged anything. The food is intact.

I direct the family and MacGee to load up as much as possible. We will need to make as few trips as possible. We manage half and the trip back takes us several days. I'm exhausted by the time we make it back to the shacks.

"Well, that was fun," MacGee says.

I'm standing with him watching the sun set. "I have no desire to go through that again," I say.

"You're telling me."

The entire trip back Sarah, who had no one to carry her, complained until Samantha lost her patience and slapped her. Sarah seemed to stare at her parents like she wanted to, and could, kill them. Her mumbling, which I hadn't heard in a while, started back up again. I'm thinking that this isn't the way a child talks, and she's only doing it since not only did her parents—who until the slap were keeping up the appearance that they would have done anything for her—physically accost her, but they're now fighting.

In fact, MacGee and I are here, at the base of the mountain, alone because of just that. Samantha and James are at it again. And though they're picking mundane things to fight about, I'm certain it's me. They've decided to chip away at each other's armor until they get to the heart of the matter.

"Maybe we should hold off on heading back there," I say.

MacGee gives me a half nod. "Well that suits me," he says in a voice that seems to be measuring me up, friendly and chiding at the same time. "Besides, it makes more sense to keep food in two separate places. Spreads out the risk and all that. You know?"

"I agree," I say, so quickly that MacGee has to smile.

Samantha's voice picks up, comes over the ground and hits me. It sounds like she's testing James to the man's limit. His voice growls back at her. I think I hear Sarah as well.

"What the hell do you think that's all about?" I ask.

MacGee's incredulous look, accompanied with a spit on the ground tells me enough.

I look up at the mountain. I can see why people in the past worshiped major landmarks like these. It feels like a messenger of the Lord. But it's all idolatry.

MacGee must have caught me staring up because he immediately asks: "So you actually climbed that thing?"

"Yeah to the top. Beautiful view. You climb much?"

He laughs. "Do I look like I climb Tom? Christ, sometimes, just when I think you're a smart boy who's got a bright future, you manage to bring me back down to earth."

I smile; the intended slight, if that's what it is, feels jovial, the kind of thing one does with a friend. Can I be friends with someone who didn't believe, who in fact mocks the Lord?

The sun is racing down to the hills, the cloud cover threatening to cover up another great sunset.

"Have you seen some of these sunsets?" I ask.

"Yeah, gorgeous things, aren't they?"

"Indeed." I pause, wondering if I should mention the Lord's hand. I don't want to keep placing a wedge between MacGee and me; I really *do* like him. Yet, who am I if I don't spread the word of God? If I am to refuse to him a chance to change his ways? Why shouldn't I mention how I see his hand in everything? Remember Jenny, I think, remember what not believing and having no hope did for her.

For a second I'm back on the edge of *that* cliff at night, the sky is clear, the stars twinkle down and the Milky Way hangs above me, smiling upon me, and there is hope in the world, in Jenny stepping away from the edge, and then I mention those last words to her and her face—which for a second was about to love me, about to fall into my arms, press against my chest, kiss my lips, talk to me, dream of a future together with me—deforms into horror, and she hates me for a split second, and I freeze wondering what it is she hates and before I can formulate a coherent thought, or react she is over the edge, and I don't peek over to see her flying, though I can see her flying in my head, instead I hear the thud, the sad sound that any other sack of material would make after being thrown off the cliff, and I look over and see her, face up, eyes open.

I never managed to get her eyes to close, even as I buried her. I want to remember her sleeping, or at least peaceful, but instead she has this look that reminds of me of the exact look that she had when she was staring at the ragged blanket after I'd first slept with her. I try to remember what it is I said to her before she jumped. What made her jump? What words could possibly have had such an effect? But I can't. It seems that something, in a moment so important, would be memorable, but it isn't.

"Tom," MacGee says, loudly.

I come back, look at him, and it takes a second for me to remember who he is, and where I am.

"You all right?" he asks.

"Yeah. Why do you ask?"

"Why do you think? You've got that stare again."

I glance about; my heart's racing. I probably shouldn't hide this from him. If there's anyone in the world whom I can talk to right now, it's him. I know this, and I also know that if I keep this inside me, I'm going to be eaten from the inside out. I won't have to worry about the insects then.

Her eyes.

"You going to tell me what that look's all about?" MacGee asks.

The mountain stares down at me, bearing witness. For the Lord, I remind myself. "It's not a nice story."

"Who has a nice story in this time and place? But you're here, aren't you?"

I don't know what that means, so I give him a confused look.

"Come on," he says, like I'm his son now. "What I'm saying is that we all, even in the past, had to survive. Pure and simple. Everything from before... was also the same; we were just better at covering up our past. And that's what happens when we decide to hide what we are, we end up doing things like this." He waves his hand over the land that's gradually darkening in the angled light.

I stare at him. I've no clue what he's saying. It feels like these are just pieces of information that he likes to release to hear himself talk. Perhaps he's just vain. I do know that he sounds like he has no more hope in life, in humanity, in God's works.

"You know," I say. "Life doesn't have to be so hopeless." I'm saying this and thinking of how exactly I will get past his intellectual defenses that he has

80

obviously put up to defend against the inclusion of hope in his life. I, after all, had been much like him for a time in my life. It'd been in college, when in the depths of learning the computer sciences, I had a professor, much like MacGee who convinced me of the futility in believing in God. What my life became, after that, however, was not something I would want to relive. I remember how Carol's warmth managed to bring me back into a righteous way of living. Nothing crazy, just a belief in Jesus. "Look." I point at the first hints of a color that the sun is starting to paint on the clouds. "How can you not see the hand of God there?"

"Oh. I'm supposed to see the hand of God in some light that has been refracted, and from that I should have hope in the entire lot of humanity? Jesus fucking Christ." MacGee spits out as he stares at the clouds.

"You don't feel the touch?" I say, not willing to give up; I really do want MacGee to be happy. "There may be science behind it, but behind that there is the Lord. Don't you feel touched by this beauty?" As if to help, as if God Himself is listening, the colors on the clouds start to spread—lighting the bottom of the clouds on fire—from one side of the sky to another, like there are two worlds, the heavens and the earth, and an eerie glow hits my face, MacGee's too, and warms my skin and soon my heart. I take in MacGee in my periphery, and he seems silent in contemplation. I decide to remain silent as this might be his moment of conversion. I remember the story of the man on his trip to Damascus. Perhaps MacGee will become the biggest believer of them all.

And the clouds drip out their light, the wind whips around; I smell MacGee's body odor, and I hope that it's the smell of a new man.

"So I'm supposed to see a sunset, and see God's hand in it? Like some chimpanzee in awe I'm supposed to be a believer in a power I can't understand, even though this is nothing but a matter of a burning ball of gas that happens to have some of its light hit the vapors floating in the air of some rock? Is that it? This," Macgee says, jabbing his finger at the ground. "Is exactly how we got into this problem. Men who couldn't think beyond some stupid morality written down by tribesmen in a desert, and the world. Was. *Thus*. Decimated."

I grind my teeth, angry that I failed, and angry that MacGee took my good graces and used them to take another stab at God. He was wrong; I knew it. The only reason people would have done something as foolish as blow everything up was because we'd moved so far away from Him, and towards the false god of reason and science. I'm not saying I'm some backward man, just that as children of God we needed to keep him in mind at all times. "That's not true."

"Oh, the man, who stares off because it's obvious that he's had to do some horrible things, is telling me that there is truth somewhere in his heart?" MacGee lets out a laugh when he finishes.

He wants to know what has been bothering me? I wonder which part of the Jenny story I should mention. I can't mention it all. "All I'm saying is that I knew someone, not too long ago, who was just like you. She... She'd lost all her faith in God. Said that there was nothing possible, and there was no future." I speak while knowing that I couldn't possibly get all the words she spoke right, but I can definitely convey the feeling she gave me, couldn't I?

"Was this before the bombs fell?"

"No." A pang of guilt hits my guts. For some reason, I remember Carol, she's still a piece of my heart, and yet I hardly think of her. Maybe she isn't the large part of my life that I knew her to be... before the bombs fell. Why? Is it that I truly loved Jenny, and not Carol? This idea weakens my resolve.

To live, to convert MacGee. I need this.

"I met her after," I say.

"How?"

Wouldn't that be great to answer truthfully?

"Ran into her after I came out of the cave. She was alone." What was a good story for her was good enough of a story for him. "Father and brother killed." I wonder if I speak with major tells, since MacGee looks into me, *deep*, when I say this. "I decided to look after her, make the promise to myself to look after her. I'd a wife before, and I think I'd like someone to take care of her, if she's still alive. You know?"

Silence. "I know."

"Then, she starts to lose hope. After all, there's no one around. She doesn't believe, and one day..." I part my hands as I speak. "She jumps a cliff. Can't take it anymore. And she's gone. This beautiful thing is done, because she had no hope." I tremble, my heart almost collapses.

Silence unwinds itself between us. I try to understand it. Perhaps it's a matter of MacGee absorbing my tale, or perhaps he expects more detail. In that uncertainty I feel like climbing to the top of the mountain, to sleep alone tonight.

"It's a fragile thing. Hope," MacGee says.

I wait for more, but I don't get anything. The darkness settles in around us. I think I hear the insects crawling underneath the ground, maybe under my skin, but it's just the wind pushing rocks aside.

The wind, like I remember reading when looking at those red formations in the Moab desert, will slowly, and patiently, shape the world with its finger. Pushing grains of sand here and there. And we humans are to make something of it. The artificial intelligence that the satellites above us possess will go on calculating what it is it had to calculate to stay on the last route it was given, and we will go on living down here. And we can't do it without hope... Perhaps there's no getting to MacGee.

The argument between Samantha and James drifts up to us. This time it pleases me, because I think of the wedge that it's creating between her and James, and that makes me think of her curves, of that thick thigh I felt, and how I would like to get it all.

No, think of God. Think of being better.

"What do you think of the smoke you saw?" MacGee asks, shaking me from my cogitation.

"I'm not entirely comfortable with it."

"Why?" he asks.

"Meeting people will have its risks. We've to know if they're friendly. Then if they outnumber us. Or can outgun us."

"Agreed. But we need to go out there and meet them. Not wait until they catch a glimpse of our fire at night and decide to come out here. When we're not in control, it *will* get messy."

I don't agree. "We'll have to be careful."

MacGee moves his jowls. "Remember one thing, Tom. I know you believe and all, but you aren't amongst friends. Even if they're Christians. The bombs, what they did was a fucked up sort of selection, though," he says quietly. "I suppose that all selection is fucked up in a way. But." He raises his voice, as if he's back from his intellectual maze. "What the bombs did was kill all the sane people, and left the people who thought Armageddon was upon us. It'll make them believe in their fucked up ways even more."

"But they *were* right," I say.

"They were," MacGee says his voice turning sad. "But they're not right in the head, not the people to lead the world."

I remain quiet. The darkness is complete. I can barely make out MacGee. I don't like his warning, even if it seems to hold some weight.

The small flames that are the chip fire start up in the distance, highlighting the facades of the shacks. A bitter cold seeps into my veins.

"We'd better head back," I say.

When we get to the fire, the family's staring at the flames dancing on their faces, highlighting their red eyes. Samantha has cried, as has Sarah. I'm not certain about James. I smile.

"So, how's everyone?" I ask and receive stabs of glares from all of them, I wonder if I went too far. MacGee lets out a croaky laugh, I relax.

"Come on people," MacGee says, smiling at Sarah. "Let's not get down on ourselves."

I sit down on the ground, expecting there to be some conversation. There isn't; there's only silence of the hurt family. Exhaustion, from the tension in the air, and the conversation and memories evoked from talking to MacGee. No one adds any more chips and the flames whimper out and soon it's nothing but embers. Everyone moves like zombies to bed. I lie down, and don't make an attempt to reach out to Samantha, if she is in fact next to me.

The memory, or rather the trail that Jenny's memory left and that last moment with her, lingers in my head. It sinks in from my brain to my heart, then my other muscles and bones, like a ravenous parasite trying to eat for which only my flesh will suffice.

This cogitation, however, I can't explain. Then the other thought that my mind had dug up, comes back to the fore. Why haven't I thought of Carol with the same intensity as Jenny? Was Carol not the light of my life? We'd done so much together. With Jenny, what had we shared? A few moments together and the rest of the time was tense hatred.

Was Carol's departure from my life not as intense? No, how can I think that? Out there in the crater that remained of Portland, I'd been sad, but I hadn't had much time to mourn, because that family of wolves came at me from nowhere.

And you killed them.

I had no choice.

I push that thought away, angry that guilt could even be associated with what I did to survive. Was that what MacGee was talking about? No, remember the Lord.

Carol. Think of Carol, why can't you think of her for more than a few seconds? I want to hurt for her. I want to cry for her.

Think.

Carol in Portland, alone, not knowing where I was, probably assumed I was dead under some rocks, or at the very least missing. Then she hears the news about one, or maybe two of the nukes. Were there any warnings? Were the people in the cities given a chance to escape? I assume that Portland was not the first city to go down. So how did she deal with it? Did she frantically try to drive away from the neighborhood? Perhaps she grabbed one of the neighbors and they decided that they'd make it out on their own. We weren't especially extroverted, but Mandy, a neighbor that went to the same church as us, was one person that Carol would've sought out. My father, would Carol have sought him out? I hope not. I loved my father, but he was a ghost of himself. Ravaged by strokes and Alzheimer's disease, I hadn't been able to do much but visit him at his home to watch him slip away from life.

And did Carol decide to make a dash for it, or did the two of them sit there and wonder if they'd done everything they wanted in life? Or perhaps they were wondering what it was I was doing. I hope that God gave her a sign to let her know I was still alive, and that there was no reason to fret about me.

Then my brain, for some reason, wonders if she even thought of me. Perhaps all she could think of was her life and how to save it.

I drift to sleep with these thoughts lingering in my mind.

The next morning I wake up late. MacGee's doing his waking up stretches, and the family is gone.

"Where are they?"

"The family? Working hard on their shrine, or so they say."

"You just wake up?"

"No, we already had breakfast."

I can't believe that they've done so much without me knowing. I keep that to myself.

"You're not helping them?" I ask.

"Why the hell would I do that?"

I laugh. And I realize that MacGee is right about at least one thing: I don't like the family just because they're Christians, like me. There was that feeling when I had felt a pull towards them, like a similar destiny, but there is still something pushing me from them. "You're a bastard, you know that?" I say with a grin.

"Hey, go build some idols with them. Seems like it goes against the hole tenant of your God," MacGee replies, a grin plastered on his face.

"Maybe." I twirl an argument in my mouth. "Well, it's keeping them quiet."

"I suppose it is."

The question lingers in the air. What else can we do? I have to keep moving. Otherwise I'll try to relive Carol's or Jenny's last moments on this earth. And thinking about the previous women in my life will cause me to think about Samantha. "You want to learn how to climb?"

MacGee looks me over like I'm out of my mind.

I poke him. "Come on old man, what else you got to do?"

"Nothing."

"And I know you don't care what happens to you, right? It's all smokes and mirrors, and what you do now doesn't matter, right? I mean it's all organic material anyways, right?"

He glares at me. "That's not what it means, though I'm sure it's what you think."

"Come on," I say as I jab him in the shoulder. "Let's go grandpa, you're not getting any younger."

I walk out and hear him coming after me.

"Tom!"

I see Sarah running as I approach the base of the mountain. I turn and she runs at me and almost knocks me over as she jumps into my arms. I pick her up and toss her.

"Sarah," I say, it's not normal to see her without her parents. "What are you doing out here?"

MacGee reaches us, and he seems out of breath. I never noticed that before, and I realize that he's trying to show that he's not fit to climb. I try not to smile.

"Sarah, princess." MacGee pauses to give Sarah a smile, to which Sarah reacts with a giggle. "How are you?"

"I'm okay," she says, almost sounding like the teenager that she'll necessarily become.

"Your parents doing well?" MacGee asks.

"They're okay." She looks down and wiggles in my arms. It's obvious that she doesn't want to talk about her parents. I give MacGee a look that'll hopefully shut him up. He looks off into the distance.

"You ready to climb?" I ask MacGee in a teasing voice.

"You're going to climb again?" Sarah asks.

"That's right. MacGee too," I add.

"Is that a fact?" MacGee says loudly.

"You're strong," Sarah says as she wraps her fingers around my biceps. "Mom says so."

"Well..." I've nothing to say to that. Sarah has just used a flirtatious voice that I haven't even heard from the likes of her mother, let alone the little girl in front of me. But since I know that it's an extension of what her mother's words, perhaps wishes, and it adds another concrete slab to the reality of Samantha wanting me, my throat dries up and I'm an animal again. All that thinking and I'm back to being an animal. I feel my heart pumping and my cock rising. Entirely inappropriate with this girl in my arms, but I'm thinking of her mother. The curves on that woman, and how, now that I know—not that one ever knows— my balls ache. God, think of God, think of what the Bible teaches.

"I want to climb," Sarah butts into my train of thought.

"We'll have to ask your parents first."

"Why?" Sarah asks.

I see MacGee flash me a smile. She is still a child.

"Because that's the way it is," I reply, knowing that it won't be enough, and that in the end, what kind of authority did I have over the child? She could climb if she wanted, and I wasn't about to find her parents to tattle on her.

"But you're stronger than them. So just tell them you let me climb, they will listen."

"I'll teach you in due time," I say, hoping that this will put her off whining for now.

"You will?" She looks me over suspiciously, though with a hint of affection. It warms my heart, reminds me that I have a little girl in my arms, and pushes away the thoughts of taking her mother.

"I will. And then you and I can watch the world together. All right?"

"Okay," she smiles and kisses me on the cheek, though dangerously close to my lips. "If you promise."

"I do."

"That's right," MacGee pats her on the head. "Uncle Tom will help you become a strong climber."

I tilt my head to show my appreciation to MacGee but, when Sarah's head is turned, he gives me a look that tells me he thinks this isn't a good idea.

"Sarah?"

"Sarah!"

Her parents call out to her. I see them as they come out of the hut. Tension still exists between them.

Sarah jumps down and runs towards them.

The family disappears back into the hut.

"You think they're just going through a fight?" I ask, hoping for something to counterbalance the ideas swirling through my head.

MacGee gives me a look that seems to tell me that I should know the answer to my own question.

"Well?" I say.

"You really don't know?"

"No."

"You're strong," says MacGee in a sexy voice.

"What do you mean?"

"I mean, remember what I said?"

"That I was protected by luck."

"You've been protected from the radiation. It's you that's causing the tension in the family."

"You think?"

"Yes, I *think*."

I want to forget this. "You ready to climb?"

"Fuck off."

"Why don't you think it's a good idea?" I ask.

"What do you mean?"

"Her climbing, you gave me a look, right?"

"She's also been weakened by the radiation. She won't be able to take it, and it will only frustrate her even more. Let her save her energy."

"You think it's a waste of energy?"

"Yep."

"And me?"

He doesn't answer.

"Quiet again, eh?"

"That's right," he replies.

I shrug and turn to the wall. The route comes back to me like an old friend's face, and I make my way up without any bad turns. When I get to the top, my forearms aren't as tired as the first time, and my mind's clean, light. There's no wind today; in fact, it's almost warm. I have the binos on me, and I check around me. In the same place there are the same smoke spirals heading up to the sky. More than before.

I lie down, rest my elbows on the ground, hold my breath, and peer through the binos. I count the smoke spirals. Ten. What are they from? They could be smoldering fires that happened naturally, or perhaps the nuclear bombs ignited some underground storage facility.

I let out my breath and try to see if there's anything else in the area.

And then I see the movement, it's quick, disappears, but it's a person—I'm sure of it. I spend twenty more minutes trying to make out what it is, but don't see anything else.

"She was staring at you again," MacGee informs me as soon as I'm back down. He hands me a meal that he's prepared from military rations, beef stew, and I scarf it down.

"Samantha?"

"That's right."

"Why are you telling me this?"

MacGee smiles.

"I saw the smoke spirals again. I'm sure there are people there."

"All right. What do you propose?"

"That we head out there and check it out. I don't like the idea of sitting around and waiting for a chance meet, which could go wrong. I want to see them and then we can make a decision on what to do."

MacGee shakes his head. "First, most normal people who aren't trying to hide something in their past are fine with staying put and not trying to keep so busy that they have to forget what they have done.

Second," he says, raising his finger in my face when I try to interject. "What are the chances that they're sending out patrols to see what's going on in the world around them? Most likely, they're just trying to survive and see another day, not search out their area. And finally, remember what I said. They could be nuts, and if that's the case, it means that they are supremely violent. Remember what the people out here are. Most are militias and the such. In fact, if you decide to dig a little further I'm sure this family wasn't out here doing a geology dig."

"Why do you think that?"

"Who brings an entire family out for a geology dig? Tell me?"

"I guess. But we can observe these people from a distance, plan a route that won't have us discovered so easily and make a decision from there. All right?"

"All right boss."

I look over at MacGee, I like that he called me that. Later on I announce to them that we are going to head out tomorrow.

That night James doesn't join us, as he's feeling sick. Things are in fact, much more jovial than they have been in a while, and I feel a strength in me that I never really felt since Jenny left me.

Samantha is giving me glances that flick at my heart and balls. Sarah's also dancing around and jumping on to me. I feel that the look she gives me is also one of a crush, but I treat it like an extension of Samantha's.

Sarah heads in. MacGee is drinking from his bottle, and I take a couple swigs. Samantha tries a sip, but coughs it back up. She leans forwards, pretending to fall, and I catch her. It's an act, but as my arm presses up on her breasts she gives me a glance.

Remember be good. Think of what you're doing to the family.

I walk off a ways to take a piss. When I'm finished I hear a crunch behind me.

I spin, thinking of the smoke spirals and the person I'm sure I saw.

"Sorry," Samantha whispers.

"Oh, it's you."

"Don't be so disappointed."

"I'm not. Where's MacGee?"

"He headed in."

I can't really make the outline of her facial features, but I can see her form, and I can smell her sex, pulsating and calling me.

My mind's blank. The only thoughts that come forth, if you can call them thoughts, are the ones that growl her name, the ones that tell me to thrust in her.

As if she senses the blood flowing through me, because I can feel it, and I can feel it move the air all around me, and I'm sure she knows it. She steps forward her arms clasp around me, then she slowly rubs my ass, my stomach, then *it*.

"I've wanted this since the day I saw you."

I feel myself in her hand, my pants have come undone and she cajoles it. I can barely control myself.

I think I hear someone walking near us, but the flame behind is out and it could be my imagination.

Take her.

Now.

I touch her hips, and thighs; I undo her pants as I rub the wet spot between her legs. I want nothing more than to meld with her, and as I stroke her body, I push into her, feel her moan.

"Not so much."

But I can barely control myself from giving her too much, even if she screams, or cries, that would be just what I want. And still I try to hold back, but the spot I've found, this home between her legs, and her mouth in my ear breathing hard, crying, or moaning, or whatever, is just the everything in my life that I've wanted. So I push and push, the gasps and her fingernails digging into me, and the climax, the burst of my gift into her. And as I curl and hold and shrink, I kiss her over and over.

When we're done and walk back to the embers, she acts like nothing happened, and me, sure I hear another rustle near us, I feel a connection to her. I don't want James to know, but then I don't want James around anymore. I want her for myself, so I can have her over and over.

The next day I wake up late. Again everyone is outside. I rustle about, moving my blanket aside, and decide that there will have to be a reckoning. The floating feeling I had with Samantha, inside her, being nothing but an animal, is no longer with me. It's as if my spirit flew for a moment, but came too close to the sun, and I fell and was crushed. What did I do? Did I not promise myself that I wouldn't? And where does Christ fit in all this?

I look up as Sarah bursts into the shack. She smiles at me. Picks up what appears to be a doll off the floor and runs back out. At least she doesn't know. To be a child and not truly understand what's going on around you.

I step out. It's a partially clear day. The clouds have cliff faces for sides and they race above us. An accompanying wind blows overhead and I see the dust kicking off the mountaintop. There will be no climbing for me today. And that's a shame, because I wanted to get as far away as possible from these people.

No one's looking at me, but I can sense something else blowing in the wind; my heart picks up its pace. I really do want to climb up that mountain. That's one thing that hasn't changed: the routes you climb, is something instinctual and can push away the worries on your mind. I look around, not wanting to be anywhere near the family, and hoping that I can get a moment with MacGee.

The wind gusts over the roofs of the shacks and blows some fine grain into my eyes. I shield my face with my arms and rub my eyes. They itch and sting like glass has been thrown in them. For some reason my mind's eye remembers the fine dust that had poured into the eyes and lungs of those people around ground zero. I almost laugh at how insignificant that moment has actually turned out to be.

All that crap about terrorists and *we* destroyed everything. How funny is that? And here we are a new beginning, and no one I've met really knows how we got into this mess, all it is is every single person using it as an excuse to throw their own personal beliefs where there should be facts. Have things really changed?

The dust still eats away at my eyes. It could be, I think, that we're fooling ourselves. Maybe all this dust in the air, ashes from a nuclear war, will just eat us away and leave not a single human alive.

After a while I'm able to look up. No one has come over to me to greet me for the day. I feel like leaving the family again.

I see Samantha bent over brushing Sarah's hair. Samantha is wearing what she always wears, those tight fitting jeans and a sweater that her breasts still manage to peek out of. Sarah looks a lot like her mother, and I realize that she's starting to grow her secondary sexual characteristics. When did this happen? I rub my eyes. MacGee is talking to James about something. James isn't looking over at me, but neither is he trying to ignore me. Samantha is making sure not to look over at me either, but she does it so naturally that I sense that our secret will always be safe.

But will it?

Is it possible that no one heard us last night? That first thrust had caught her by surprise and her gasp—almost a cry—seems like it'd traveled across the world.

And that rustle. Did I not hear the rustle?

That could have been the insects. I remember the insects and move closer to the family.

MacGee looks up at me, a half smirk on his face. "Well, look who's up? Want to eat?"

I don't answer and take the can of food he hands me. It might have been late, but MacGee and I were still supposed to head out and check out the next group of people.

"Good morning," James says.

"Good morning. You feeling better?" I reply, though I try not to say anything more, in case that gives away how bad I want to look up to Samantha at this point, as well as my beating heart, and the desire to take her.

Take her.

No.

"Much, thank you."

"We were talking about your plan," MacGee says, a smirk still on his face.

I'm sure he knows, but I'm still trying my hardest not to look up at Samantha, though it would be a stroke to my desire if I could just see her hips, that ass of hers, and ravage her with my eyes. I'm so obsessed with this lust, that I wonder if I should be worried about MacGee's labeling of the plan as mine. I look the two men over, they're no threat, I remind myself.

"What about it?"

"We're considering the risk," James says.

I bite into the can's contents. It's slightly bitter, but that could be because it was stale and old. I look at MacGee who gives me another cheery smile. And the voice picks up; it's very possible that they, even old MacGee, can poison me. Wasn't walking in on them just now like walking in on a group of people who'd known each other for a long time? From all the things that MacGee said, he can't be on these people's side. He's your friend, remember that.

"And what about the risk?" I ask, finishing the food in the can and tossing it to the ground. I half-expected to see insects, but there were none.

"We're thinking that now might not be a good time to meet up with more people," MacGee says.

"I thought we agreed to do it," I say, a little angry that MacGee has changed his mind without me.

"Listen to me," MacGee says with his hand out to me, like he's trying to soothe me. "We're thinking that it's almost winter, right? People must be trying to get ready for the time when there'll be no more food."

"Getting ready for what? There's no harvesting. People have as much food as they'll ever have. Besides, we're not meeting them; we're going to check them out. Make sure they're not a threat. All right?"

"Listen, we go out there, and there's a high chance that they'll sniff us out," James says, though he says it in such a whiney voice that I couldn't be angry with him.

Or at least I shouldn't have been, but my anger was rising up again. I beat it down. Remember how Jesus was able to overcome with his works. Remember. I make sure not to glance up at Samantha.

"Sniff us?" I ask.

"Yeah, haven't you noticed that you can smell a person a mile away? There aren't any other smells to compete with it. The world is basically dead," James says.

"Yeah," MacGee says. "Before you two came up on me I was sure I could smell life. I was too tired to look around, but I ended up being right. Anyone with more wherewithal should be able to sniff you out from miles away. All right?"

I think for a second. "How far away could you smell us?" I ask MacGee.

"I smelled the fire from at least a mile. It was something that tickled my mind, and I thought, all right I'll head towards that area near the tall mountain. My smell, by the way." He raised his finger as he spoke, like he always did before he made a point. "Was eaten away by an explosion, seared the inside of my nose and left me with half the capacity of a normal person."

"You didn't have good smell for most of your life then?" I ask.

"That's exactly it," MacGee replies.

"So you must have been one stinking bastard, eh?" I jab MacGee when I say it, breaking out a grin.

For a split second, MacGee's face appears hurt. "You bet." MacGee lets out his rusty laugh.

"No wonder you went it alone in the mountains," I say.

I see James crack a smile, and now I'm certain that he doesn't know about me and his wife. That cuts some of the tension inside me, though I make certain not to look up at her.

"No, it wasn't that, at that point, because of the lack of smell, I'd been with such questionable." MacGee pauses mid-sentence to sneak a peek at the two women and he leans forward to whisper: "Pussy that I was being chased out of every town for what I done." He finishes with another snort and leans back to roar the rest of his laugh. At the same time a fart lets lose.

James and I join in with him. Now I sense that they were right about not seeking other people.

"What are you men laughing about there?" Samantha looks over with a smile.

"Oh nothing, honey, just some jokes," James replies.

I love the smile on her face, it is indeed enticing, and though I lick it up with my eyes in a second, I also manage to absorb her thighs and that place between her legs where I found that oh so comfortable home. My member bulges and I make sure to pick up the can I'd thrown down and scrape it for food. I'm pleased to notice that the tension that had been so prevalent the past few days between James and Samantha is now gone. In fact, the smile she flashed, it'd been for him.

"Well, don't leave us out, that would be rude," Samantha says.

"Oh..." MacGee grins. "I don't think the little one wants to hear an old man's tales."

"And." I jump in unable to hold myself back, even though my brain is telling me not to speak to Samantha, especially not in front of James because something in our conversation will leak out the truth.

"He means 'tails' when he says 'tails'." I look away and at MacGee so that nothing is given away between Samantha and I.

MacGee chuckles. "He's right."

"Oh, is that right?" Samantha says.

I feel something in her tone and glance up at her. Starting in my guts, I freeze up. I feel her eyes drilling through me, and again blood starts flowing, like she's a witch and can control me to her whims. The worst thing about this is that she seems to be so cool and calm that I'm not even certain if this is the same woman as last night. "Yeah," I barely manage to say.

"I'm old enough to hear this, and so is Sarah."

MacGee and I settle our eyes on James.

"Honey," James says with a voice that is firm enough not to belong to him. "MacGee here." He pats MacGee and smiles. "Was talking about some questionable women he... eh... had."

"MacGee." Samantha tilts her head at him and touches his elbow. "Well, aren't you the old hound dog?"

MacGee glances away from her and down at the ground. "I was young once."

I enjoy MacGee's blush, or at least assumed blush, it gives me some room to hide the ravenous blush I myself am experiencing all over my body.

"And you Tom?"

I look up and all there is are her eyes, or not exactly her eyes but the effect that wavers off them and hits me, square in the chest, and the world around her is trembling. This is in fact not a visual effect, but something I feel, and I can see or feel the curves on her body, like something that's a part of my body, like knowing your arm is there, though it's behind your back, and this is how I see and feel her,

101

as if our bodies are fusing together; my heart racing, and my pores glistening.

"Me?" I say slowly, as if the words are some foreign language I'm trying to learn.

"Yes. Have you ever had questionable women?"

I feel everyone look at me. How do I answer this, and why is she teasing me in front of everyone? In front of her husband, of all people!

"Yeah, ever had a questionable woman?" MacGee asks as if to prod me on.

I should have something smart to say, it's not that hard of a question to deflect, but knowing my audience, knowing the secret that two of us share, is all that my mind can juggle and as a result I can't even think of what to say.

"How can you have a woman?" Sarah breaks the silence, looking at all of us like we're the silly ones. "That doesn't sound right."

"Well, kind of like me and you father," Samantha says.

"Oh," Sarah replies, though she doesn't seem satisfied with the answer.

That break is what I need to recoup my brain cells and give an answer.

"Well?" Samantha asks, like she wants to see me squirm.

"I'd say every woman is questionable, and every woman wasn't."

There's a pause.

MacGee lets out a laugh and slaps me on the back. "Ain't that the truth."

The others chuckle along, though Sarah is obviously confused.

"How about you?" MacGee taps James on the knee. "You get too many questionable women before you met the light of your life?"

"No," James says with a smile and glance at Samantha that evokes in me a spot of guilt so strong I feel an acidic build up in my heart. "Samantha was the first woman I ever kissed, and will be the last."

Samantha smiles back at him. It's genuine; I even see her eyes glistening. I want to see her squirm. It's foolish, but the words left my mouth before I could coral them back in: "And you, Samantha, you ever have a questionable man?"

"I wouldn't call James questionable," she says, without hesitation.

"I was her first and last kiss as well," James shoots out, defensive.

"That's right," Samantha says, patting down Sarah's hair. The couple embrace, and I'm jealous. I feel MacGee's stare on my face. He tilts his head. It could mean "well there you have it" or "don't do anything crazy" and I feel like I want to break the couple up and take Samantha in front of them all. Except it's obvious that the woman is extremely smart and willing to say anything to get what she wants. She would cut me down to size if she wanted.

"I suppose you two have a point about not heading out there to meet up with some unknowns," I say.

"Good."

The couple stops and sits down, hand in hand. It's the first time that I've really seen them this intimate. I keep quiet and play the game of not looking at her. I manage to convince everyone that we should have someone at certain intervals, checking the area around us, in case someone indeed has decided to move in on us. James claims to know how to set up traps so I tell him he should set them up, and we should make a map of the place.

Us three men set about making the map. James shows us how to make the traps. They're simple holes to dig, place a sharp object at the bottom, then cover it up so that no one can see. We use some pipes I gathered from Bill's place, and pieces of a tarp to cover it up, throwing soil and rocks on top of that. It seems pretty good to me. We make sure that we memorize the placements. No need to get caught in our own traps.

As James and MacGee work on a larger trap, I head back to the shacks to grab some food. When I make my way back, there's no one there. I'm sure I hear Sarah giggle, but I pay no attention to where she can possibly be. When I enter the shack where we sleep I see Samantha standing over my bed.

She hasn't heard me so I look around to make sure that Sarah is in fact not around and sneak up behind her. She does a small jump when I wrap my hands around her waist.

"No," she says timidly. The woman who'd just earlier tried to make me squirm in front of her husband is no longer here.

"Yes." I kiss the back of her neck. It's soft, and tastes clean, even though it's not.

I turn her around and look into her eyes. There is none of the lust that I'm sure I felt the previous night. For some reason this makes me furious. I want to take it, but I won't. "What?" I say, angry.

"It's just that..."

"What? You came to me, didn't you?"

She nods silently. "I don't want to hurt him."

"Don't worry," I say, and I look into her eyes, those glistening things and I'm sad that I won't get much satisfaction, but I'm glad that she decided to confide in me about something. And it feels like that's more filling than anything else I've experienced in a while.

That night, as the sun sets, I stand near the base of the mountain with MacGee. The family is in the shack, polishing up their shrine.

"I talked to James, found out a little bit more about him," says MacGee.

"Is that right. Anything good?" I ask. I'm still apprehensive about their relationship.

MacGee takes a sip of his moonshine and passes it on to me. "I confirmed my initial suspicions."

"About?"

"He was no geologist. He was in his view, but he was out here trying to find evidence that was contrary to evolution."

"On his own dime?"

"No, some Christian Science institution that pays quacks like him to contradict science."

"Oh," I say. "Well, does it matter that he wanted to find some holes in a theory?"

"It's *not* a matter of finding a hole in a theory. People like him were just about finding something to be used for propaganda so that they could convince other dimwits to move away from science. I'm telling you, it's this movement away from science that caused this whole fall."

"You're wrong about that," I say pointedly, taking the flask and downing the burning liquid down my throat. "It was not God that did this. It was the devil."

"Oh the devil," MacGee says with a sneer on his face.

"What does it matter if he wanted to find a hole in the theory?" I say, exasperated that MacGee is choosing to be so close-minded about this. "Besides, whether or not evolution is correct does nothing for us. That James knows how to make traps does."

MacGee lets out air in a puff and shakes, as if he cannot understand my point of view. "The traps are helpful, but what about what comes after this?"

"Why does that matter? You yourself said that it was pointless, right?"

"You didn't understand me then," MacGee replies. I get the sense that he's getting angry.

"Explain."

"Don't you want to build towards something that our children will be proud of?"

"You mean rebuild America?" I ask.

"Exactly. Rebuild civilization again."

"What's that got to do with James' beliefs? Or mine." I tap my chest. The sun's now falling; there's a crack in the clouds, and it looks like an ominous puffy cliff, the light highlighting shadows on this cliff face so that the texture almost seems like it belongs to another world. I smell something; it's not MacGee or I, because our smells are close, but it's far away, as if I can smell people from another mountain. I brush this off; it could be the family.

"Listen, what was America all about?"

I open my mouth to speak, then shut it. The words I was going to use seem foolish, platitudes— even fanciful. What *was* America all about? Freedom? It seems like that is too superficial a rubric to use. After all, comfortable suburban living doesn't seem to be the right answer.

"I'll tell you what it was," MacGee says, after the wind picks up and dies down again. "It was about enlightenment, about providing a place to move people forward with the best ideals possible. Freedom to do what they want, of course, but with the reins of making the country the best place for dreams to be lived out. And science was the best vehicle for this. Remember that."

I remain still; what MacGee has said is indeed catchy, but was it true? What is it about the word freedom that I don't like? There has to be a correct answer out there somewhere. I look down and kick some of the dirt and ash mix that my boots rest on. In the ashes lies the answer. The reason we went to war, destroyed everything will be have to be known to find out how to improve the nation. I want to say this to MacGee, but for some reason I stay quiet, it also seems foolish.

"I will," I say.

"You agree?"

"I don't know MacGee. How can a person figure anything out when we only truly know so much? You say science is the best vehicle, and yet that sounds like a belief, like you want a god, but decided to choose a different one than me and James. So why piss on ours?"

"You're not listening to me. Forget the science bit," MacGee says. "What about the reason for our nation? For any nation. Don't you agree?"

I stop thinking about MacGee because I'm sure I smell that distant smell of someone. I think that maybe it's the family, but I'm pretty sure I know what they smell like. My body tightens up; the voice speaks, it tells me to get ready for a fight.

"Tom? You with me?"

Oh yes, the nation. The reason for being. I'm still not certain. "I agree with you. It's a vehicle so that people may live as they choose," I say, still thinking about the smell more than the conversation at hand.

"That's fair enough, a life to choose on your own. But here's the thing, and the reason you have to be wary of the likes of James, and most likely the other people who survived this war."

"What's that?" I ask, feeling tension in my heart.

"They won't allow others to do as they choose, it's the very nature of religion."

"That's only the extremists," I reply, once again forgetting the smell and getting annoyed at MacGee for going back to the same thing over and over.

"No, it isn't. It was in our country before the nukes fell, but that's only because they were winning. If these people decide that they are losing they will lash out harder at every perceived enemy. It's inherent."

"I think you're thinking about Muslim extremists, not Christians."

"No, that's just it; it's the same thing, both are violent, especially when given the chance. People are just that way."

That last sentence burrows into my head and starts to eat away at me. "All people are inherently violent?" I think about all the things I was still trying to forget. "Is that it?" I ask. Guilt creeps up and I fight it back.

"People are animals."

"Then why does it matter what they believe?"

MacGee doesn't answer me. He's looking at the cloud, formed above us like a mountain about to fall on our heads. "That's amazing, isn't it?"

The sun is close to setting, and the facture that it highlights on this cloud is such a mixture between soft and hard, that I know I'm witnessing something that only God can create. "It is."

I stare at this wall of clouds shifting, always changing, and yet keeping the same form. The wall above seems so detailed that I feel like I could reach out and touch it, and yet that it's so far away makes me mourn that I could never fly amongst those swirls of puff. Thinking about this separate world makes me think of what I've done. What of what MacGee said? Isn't he right? What have I done before this moment of peace in the bosom of this family? And what have I done with that peace? Tried to tear them apart by falling for Samantha, by lusting for her. Was I not evil?

Sitting here, thinking about that, the peace that I've finally attained, the ability to sit next to a person and be perfectly still and not worry about what they were going to do, only makes the recent past that much more clear in my mind: Please... Don't. The words that a man spoke before I blew his brains out. Then I proceeded to take his sister. Take her. Took her. And the last look *she* gave me was one of absolute horror. Are we all simply organic animals waiting to exploit one another?

"Did you mean what you said about people being made to do evil things?" I ask.

"I was just talking."

Has the beauty of the sun set dug into MacGee's thoughts?

"So you don't believe that?"

He lets out air. I wait.

"I do," he says. "I do."

"Have you ever done something evil?"

"Evil?"

"Yeah, I say.

He doesn't answer. I forget him for a second, looking at the wall in the sky getting darker and darker, until it's nothing but a shadow. A hit of overwhelming sadness hits me. This is it, isn't it? If He is above, how will He judge me? Did I not do the best I could?

"Not evil. I've done some bad things in my days. Nothing I would call evil," MacGee says, finally breaking the silence with his words, shattering my hope that he and I will have more in common. Am I willing another person to commit things as I have just so I can have someone else to suffer with?

"Like what?" I ask.

"I shot down people. In the wars before. Skirmishes, really."

"What do you mean people? You mean innocents?"

He doesn't reply.

I feel like that's enough of an opening.

"Before I came here, there was a woman." I am already lying. Is this how I'll always be? "Girl, really, though I'm not sure about her age."

"Right before you came here?"

"Yup. I..." I stop. The flask; I pick it up and drink it. The liquid burns my throat, settles in my stomach like a rock. It makes me feel better, hoping that it'll burn a hole in my stomach. "Before her I ran into some guys. Two guys." I can feel my throat shrink, and it's not from the moonshine. Should I tell him everything? And if not him, then who? I can feel him next to me, still, waiting for some sort of explanation.

"They came at me. I really didn't have a choice. I..."

"Did what you had to do," MacGee says.

"Right. Only they were her father and brother."

"Oh," MacGee says and takes the flask, taking a swig from it.

"I never told her."

"Of course."

"Lied to her about them, in fact. Though I wonder to this day if she knew," I say.

The darkness of the sky is underway. The clouds are only black orbs in an ever-blackening pool. Soon it will all be dark. I smell feces somewhere.

"She killed herself. And it was most likely because of..." I say.

MacGee doesn't reply. Could I have said too much?

I want to say: "She didn't believe in God, MacGee. She had no hope for the future of the human race. Don't turn out like her. Just don't." Instead I look to the dark outline of the earth contrasting with the sky and clouds, and wait for MacGee to answer.

"Don't let it weigh on you, Tom. You can't blame yourself for things that are out of your control."

"Was I evil?"

"No. Evil is something else. You're not it."

"Do you even believe in evil?" I ask, knowing that it's uncalled for, but I can't help it.

"It's not you Tom. That's all you need to know. You survived and that's what matters in the end. Just survive. All right?"

It sounds like a plea, and I wonder why he doesn't include himself, or the rest of the family in this.

We're surrounded by darkness, and though I haven't divulged everything to MacGee, the fact that I at least unloaded something and he's accepted that, means a lot. I want to hug him, tender, to show him how much it means. I don't, though.

"Thanks for listening," I say.

"Of course," he says and pats me on my back. "What are friends for?"

I like the sounds of us being friends.

"You ever feel like you need to talk about something else, let me know. I'll be glad to listen. No matter what it is. All right?"

"Same for you," I say.

"Of course. But I don't think I'm carrying the same crosses as you."

I stay quiet.

"And if you want to be quiet, that's fine too. You got it? Whatever it is, though, I'm not going to judge you."

"Why not?"

"It's not my character."

He was just judging James pretty harshly. I decide to let it be.

"Fair enough," I say.

"I know what I said about god and all might get to you, but that's me and my world view. It has nothing to do with us. Our friendship is more than that."

"All right," I say, though it doesn't make much sense.

"Good. I don't want you to think that I'll ever judge you."

"Fine," I say wondering why he's stressed this so much. It has, though, made me more comfortable. He gets up. I get up with him. He places his hand on my shoulder, and we embrace.

Footsteps make their way to us.

"What are you two doing up here?" It's Samantha.

"Just talking," MacGee says, as he steps back from me.

"Looks like it's a little more than that." She's carrying a lantern that runs on fuel that we don't have much of. I want to tell her to put it out.

MacGee chuckles. "No, it isn't."

"Hi, Tom," she says.

I tremble. I want her in my arms. I want her whispers in my ear. "Hi Samantha." I can smell her. It's distinct and sharp, and it only makes me want to love her more.

The silence that settles in makes MacGee shuffle his feet. "James and Sarah still up?" he asks.

"No, James isn't feeling good again, and neither is Sarah. They went to bed early."

"Must be a bug, or something," I say.

"Something," she says.

"I'm tired," MacGee says. "Good talking to you Tom." He pats me on the shoulder again and walks down to the shacks. I stare on at the dust trail in his wake.

The wind picks up, and I feel Samantha a few feet away. The lantern is down by her knees and is highlighting her thighs, that place between her legs. Blood rushes. I try to calm myself down. I want to have that moment again where she showed a part of her soul to me.

"You're wasting fuel," I say.

She places the lantern down, but it's still on. She looks at me, or at least I think she is, because her eyes are a shadow, as is her face. Only the tips of her lips and nose are highlighted.

She kneels down and turns off the lantern. We are in a world of nothing. Just me and her. I step towards her; she does the same and takes my hand. All that desire to have a piece of her soul is slowly giving way to the want of her. Or it. Barbaric lust. What was I?

113

"I'm sorry about earlier," she says.

My hands testing her curves, the lust is too strong. It's cold all around us, but we are each other's warmth, the sacs of fervor holding out until the universe decides to push in and make us cold too. But for now there is heat and there is desire and I want nothing more than to feel the passion of the now.

I reach underneath her shirt. Her skin trembles beneath her clothes. Her hands grip my arms. I take her to the ground, and we tremble. Her clothes off, I feel her warmest part, enter, and we shudder together.

Lying next to each other, her close to me, I want to ask her about what she said earlier, but I can't find the strength to do so, because it might put space between us, and I don't want to be alone. Not right now.

"What were you two talking about?" she asks, her head on my chest.

"Nothing, really. Just about his views on God. Mine." Why didn't I want to open up to her when I expected her to open up to me? "Some things I did before I came here. I... had to survive, I suppose."

She traces her finger over my face.

Instead of replying she plays with me, pulling, using her tongue, and finally we meld again. I feel her insides, and she whispers in my ear, not words, but desires, and it's not long before I tense up and finish.

I wait for her confessions, but I receive none. That action of hers, the fact that maybe she doesn't care to confide in me, pulls at my lungs, takes the words from my mouth, and makes me feel hollow, where only a moment ago I was floating in the air. I want to beg for some sort of answer, but I don't. She might just need some time to open up to me.

She walks back to the shacks. I wait, staring at the black sky, before the cold finally gets to me, and I head back as well. Before I enter the shack I wonder about her, and why it is I want her so badly. Is it because of everything that I couldn't have with Carol, or Jenny? The things that I'm missing out on because those women are no longer with me, and I need to find those things with Samantha? I'm not sure and in that uncertainty I want her even more. I don't know why but it feels stronger than anything I felt for those two women. With Samantha, right now, I'm swimming with the knowledge that I would burn the world for her; kill everyone in it for her. Was that love? Wasn't that love? What was love, if not that?

I wake up the next morning, and this time no one else is awake. I wait until someone stirs, James as it turns out, before I decide to get out of my bundle of blankets. We're going to need a better plan before real winter settles in.

Everyone is up and eating outside when I smell something again. It was what I smelled the previous night, and it scares me. It is definitely not any one of us that's omitting it. Could it be the insects?

"Anyone smell that?" I ask.

MacGee stops eating to shake his head.

James and Samantha shake their heads as well.

"I smell something odd."

"Sorry," MacGee says, and waves the air behind him.

Sarah and Samantha giggle. James gives me an odd look. It's for what I'm saying, not the night before, I tell myself. There's no way he knows.

"No, I really do smell something," I say.

"Like what exactly?" asks MacGee.

I pause to think out what exactly I smell. It felt like a constantly moving object, and it's something that scares me. "Like other people are here," I say.

James looks at me. "You think?"

"I know," I say, my nerves getting frayed again. Something tells me this won't be so clean. It won't be like when we met up with MacGee. It's going to be like before, I think. I reach in my pants. My handgun isn't there.

"How far are they?" MacGee asks.

I look at him. "How should I know?" I pause; the smell is getting stronger. Like there are a lot of people. How *should* I know? I've never used my smell to judge how far away anything is. "I think they're close." The wind shifts and the smells become clearer. "Everyone get ready," I say and walk back in the shack to grab my handguns and rifle.

I'm apprehensive, but I also know what to do. Be quick, and don't hesitate. I've come out on top so far; will I come out on top again?

The others follow me, grabbing their guns. I look at Samantha who kisses James.

"You two should stay here," I say.

"No," Samantha replies.

"She's right," James says. "If there're people, and they're hostile, it'll do the women no good to hide. They'll have to fight too."

"And if there are lots of people we're going to need all the firepower we can get," MacGee added.

I need to keep my mouth shut. I feel protective of Samantha. I chide myself; I had better not be falling in love with a woman who's already taken.

Outside the shack I wait for the others. I don't want to walk anywhere alone and leave my back exposed and get surprised again.

"Ready?" MacGee asks. He's right behind me.

"Let's move," I say. And we walk up to the base of the mountain, trying our best to keep low.

When we get to the base of the mountain the smell is overwhelming me. I look over at either side. I don't see anything. My nostrils, however, are burning with the presence of people, everywhere. The family joins us. I nod my head at them. "Keep low."

I'm thinking about the direction of the spirals. If people came from there, they'll be climbing up the side I'm looking down. The other side, the one facing the cave, I point Sarah and Samantha to keep an eye on. That should keep them out of harms way.

"Spread out," I tell MacGee and James. They listen. "No one else smells anything?"

They shake their heads. I start to doubt myself. Am I just confused? I look at the rocks that make up the hillside. Somewhere amongst the rocks are people, but if we're to head down there, we'll lose the high ground. What then?

I get behind a rock and wait. The others follow my actions, though I'm not sure why they're listening to me. After what seems to be nearly an hour, the others shuffle, agitated. We can't stay here forever. Perhaps a guard will work?

MacGee is the first one to move and he walks by James, whispering to him for a second before he crouches next to me.

"You still smell them?" he asks.

"That's right," I reply, though I'm not that certain about my nose anymore.

"No one's moving if they're here," MacGee says, his voice laced with the possibility that they might not be anywhere near here.

"I know. It probably sounds nuts, but I can smell them. Almost as well as I can smell you, or James."

"Or Samantha," he gives me a grin when he says this.

I look at him, does he know? He made himself sparse very quickly last night. Those pauses between me and Samantha might have been too obvious. I look over at James who's looking at the hillside intently, a little too intently. "What does he think?"

"Don't worry about him," MacGee says. "If you smell something, I believe you, all right?"

"Thanks," I say. It means a lot, him trusting in me and my instinct.

"But we can't stay here forever, wouldn't make sense. Right?"

"Right, but if they're here, and they're hiding, then we can't stay in the shacks, because then we'll be sitting ducks."

"That's true," MacGee says, shaking his head and looking over the rock and to the hillside. "Maybe we can leave a guard here. You know, someone who'll keep an eye. They'll have a gun, and so if they see someone they can fire in the air, warn us. That way we won't be caught with our pants down."

I nod.

"I'll take the first shift," MacGee says.

We let James know; then James and I go and collect Samantha and Sarah, who both haven't seen a thing. In fact, when we see them Samantha is sitting on a rock, Sarah between her legs, and braiding Sarah's hair. "We ready to go?" Samantha says with such acid on her tongue, that I'm sure I want to punch her. I keep it in.

Back at the shacks the family goes at the shrine, working harder than they normally do, as if their time is limited.

I sit in the middle of the shacks, wondering what it is that I smell, even now. Was I going crazy.

Sarah runs out and at me. She stops a few feet away. Instead of being warm and loving, she's keeping her distance. It must have been her parents talking about me.

Nelson Lowhim

"Hi," she says.

"Hi there."

"Do you still smell something?"

"Yes," I say, feeling like I'm about to walk into a trap that will remind me of the childish pranks I endured when I was in school.

"What does it smell like?"

"People."

"Lots of them?"

"Yes."

"But we can't see them?" she asks this last question with a wary look in her eyes.

"That's right."

A long pause, she's examining me with short glances from her feet.

"Are you crazy?" she asks.

I should brush this off, after all, she is a child, but just the possibility that Samantha might have planted this idea in her head makes me flush, tense. "Who said that?"

"No one. I was just asking," she says, her eyes now darting between my chest and her feet.

"Sarah!" Samantha peeks her head from the shack doorway and looks at me for a second. The look is not friendly. I wonder if she turns into another person at night, if the woman I love is some lustful demon that can only survive when the sun is down.

Sarah turns and runs back at her mother.

Samantha looks at me one more time. "By the way, if you're the one doing all the smelling, you can pull guard for all of us. I'm not wasting my time up there with your silly ideas."

Before I can retort she ducks into the shack, and I think I hear giggling.

Her words cut me hard. My cheeks flush.

I get up, my handguns in my hand and walk to where MacGee is keeping guard. I don't need another moment with the family, or the succubus that Samantha has turned into.

As I'm making it up to where MacGee is pulling guard I hear a thud, like someone being hit in the chest. I pull out my handgun and run.

"Sorry Tom. He snuck up on me."

I see MacGee with a wiry, rat-looking man, almost black with grime, holding a gun to his head.

I raise my handgun. This shouldn't be a hard shot; the thing was to make sure that I didn't think. Just shoot.

"Don't," the man says.

"Let him go then," I say. I can smell him clearly now, and I know that it was him that I smelled all along.

"Sorry, he can't do that," a voice behind me says.

I spin. There are three other dirty men there. I smell them as well.

I smell more, almost overwhelming my senses. I turn. There are now five men, maybe women, far too covered with dirt for me to tell. Not all of them have guns, some have axes and spears. I wonder if I can take them all out.

"Don't even think about it." Another man has stepped forward off to the side. He has a booming voice; it vibrates my chest when he talks, even though he's several feet away from me. He's tall, long and wiry, but with enough muscle that I wouldn't call him skinny. He's not dirty, and the others seem to look at him, as if for guidance. I assume he's the leader. Perhaps shooting him will do. I point my handgun at him.

"Let go of my friend. What do you want?"

The man looks me over. His eyes, blue, maybe with a mix of brown, or green, grab my face, and I breathe in deeply so that I can stare him back down and not look away.

"That sounds fair. Let him go," the man says.

They let MacGee go.

I lower my handgun. "Thank you."

The man is looking me over, as if I'm some alien, but I feel that there's a level of respect in his eyes. "You're welcome," he says.

"What are we going to do with 'em?" says a man or woman, I can't tell because the voice is high-pitched, behind me asks.

"You don't do anything," I say out loud.

The booming man smiles. "You've got balls. I like that."

A nervous tittering from his men arises behind me. I wonder what they want. Though the man in front of me doesn't seem to harbor any ill intentions, I know I've misjudged people before, so I'm trying not to be too trusting.

"What do you want?" I ask.

"Well, we're going to have to ask you and your friend, and any other friends you may have, a few questions."

"No one's asking any questions."

"We will," the man says, as if he's brushing off a child's request. "We outnumber you, after all. So we'll ask all the questions we want."

He holds that stare, and I stare right back. I'm back to thinking about what it is I'll have to do to shoot all of them. MacGee is without his gun, and he's too old to be of much use. I'll take just the booming man out, if I have to. "The fuck you will."

He acts as if he's exasperated. "Come out, everyone."

And they crawl out. I lose count, but I'm sure there are at least twenty of them. None of them look as imposing as the leader here, but there are enough people to put a damper in my plans. I decide I need to temper my attitude, but I won't give up my gun, no matter what.

"Now do you understand?" he asks.

Sarah's giggling pierces the tension between me and the man. He looks over.

"Go get everyone," he says to a few of his men. Then he looks at me. "How many more are there?"

"Just three," I say without thinking.

Within minutes the family is with us.

"What's the meaning of this?" James asks.

I feel like telling the family that I told them so, but it doesn't seem like the most important thing at the moment. I'm not so certain if we're going to live to see another day.

"Let me ask you something. And this is really the only real question I have: do you believe?" he asks the last part with more force and volume than anything he's said so far, and with a voice like his, it booms, shakes my head. "In the Lord? Do you believe in the savior Jesus Christ? That he died for our sins?"

"We do," James says, quickly; Samantha agrees with him with a few furious nods. "We do believe."

The man tilts his head. "Good. I believe you. And you?" he asks, turning his face to me.

I don't feel like groveling. "Not any of your business. Besides, you're a stranger; what's your name, *stranger*?"

The man pauses like he doesn't believe me, as if I've thrown something in his face. "You certainly *are* brave."

"Just tell him, Tom," James says.

"Yeah." A dirty man, the one who had the gun to MacGee's head pokes me with his gun. He does it with a slow movement that gives me enough confidence to grab the barrel of his gun, when its line of sight no longer includes me, and pull it out of his hands.

"Yeah what?" I say, pushing the man to the ground and hold him there. He's weak.

At least five guns are cocked and pointed my way.

"You really are braver than you are smart, aren't you?" the booming man asks.

"Well, I was raised with some level of manners. I'm Tom, by the way. What's yours?"

He looks at me for a few seconds before realizing that I'm serious. I'm not even certain about what I'm doing; all I remember is how useless begging is, from either side of the gun.

"Fair enough," he says. "Lower your weapons."

His men listen to him without hesitation. I let go of the man I pushed down, and hand him his gun. The man takes his gun back from me as he gets up, glaring at me like he'll soon put a knife in my back.

"I'm John," the tall man says and extends his hand.

I step forward and shake his hand. He has a firm grip, but he's still weaker than me—I'm sure of that. What MacGee told me rings through my head.

"Well Tom, we certainly have been rude."

"That's fine. Just think we should watch out for the rudeness. Right?" I say.

"So are you a believer?"

"Of course," I say, and as I roll the words out of my mouth, I remember that MacGee isn't a believer. Surely he knows better than to profess his true beliefs here?

"And you?" John looks over to MacGee.

"I am not," MacGee says.

"Listen." I step between the man and MacGee. "He's got a few loose ideas, but who doesn't?"

John sizes me up. "All right. We'll keep an eye on him."

John, it turns , is the leader of the group. A group numbering at close to fifty people. Men and women. He tells me this as he has convinced us to come back to his place. He claims to have farming, and electricity. I'm eager to see, the family too; only MacGee is hesitant. I convince him to come, he'll be under my protection, I say. In the end, I don't think he has a choice.

John has decided to take me under his wing. And though I don't much like listening to people, I remember what MacGee and I'd talked about with regards to the building towards something new. To rebuild America. I don't like everything about John but I understand that the best way to do this is to gather the largest group possible and build from there.

We load up the sleds, spread out the food and any important items amongst those in the group and we march on. I'm in the middle with John. There is his inner circle a little further out, and then the rest of the people are behind that. The family and MacGee are part of that last group. I don't mind not being around them.

John is interesting.

"So where were you when the bombs fell?" I ask.

"We were living like we always did. Living without sin out here. We knew the Lord was going to speak to the human race sooner or later. It was only a matter of time and then He did. And He let the believers, like us," John says this last part with a gesture of his hand to show he includes me and him in this group. "Live, while He punished the others."

I wonder if what MacGee said is true. Is he a nut? Some end of the world man who just happened to be lucky? I keep quiet. Mainly because I like John, and I also know that confronting him won't be in my best interests—not right now at least.

"We have to build a new world, one that will not forget the Lord," he says.

"I agree," I say; happy that he's speaking about something I believe. "I think we lost our way before."

"Exactly," John says. "You know when I first saw you, and saw how you were acting, I knew you had the Lord in your heart."

"You too," I say, not sure if he's lying. When I'd done what I did, it hadn't been with God in my mind.

"Thanks," Johns says, with enough soft overtones that I wonder if that's his weakness: flattery.

I remember the other question that had been on my mind. "Tell me, why was it the bombs fell? What's the story behind it?" I ask. I'm very sure that if someone knew, it would be him.

"Why do you ask?"

I tell him my story.

"So God truly did protect you," he says, his head shaking.

I smile. "I truly am blessed," I say. I like that he agrees with me on this matter.

"That you are. The reasons the bombs fell are much because of what you said. We as a country

126

forgot about God. We continued on our path with the devil and this is what happens when you decide to forget the Lord," John sweeps his hand across the land. "He lets us know how truly is the most powerful."

I feel comfortable in John's presence. He's way of talking, so certain and assured, lets me know we've made the right decision in coming here. I also know that he's smart enough to hold a conversation with.

"So we'll build another nation that will continue America's traditions. The way they were intended. Right?"

"That's right. But it will be even more than that, Tom," John says. "We are to build His Kingdom here and wait for the King of Kings to return. That, after all, is our reason for being. Is it not?"

"It is."

It takes a few days to walk back, given the weight we have on our backs. I impress all of John's men by being able to carry more than anyone. I even carry Sarah when she's too tired to walk. Samantha gives me a glance of desire. But I'm too angry with her for the slights she leveled at me to give her anything back in return. James, for some reason, seems to be more and more out of it. MacGee also seems to be sick at best. I try to talk to him, but he brushes me off. I wonder why this is, but don't dwell on it. Everyone is quiet by the time we arrive at the compound.

John offers us a place in the middle of the compound. He claims it's a place of honor for us, but part of me thinks that this is really his attempt to keep an eye on us. The compound is quite the refugee camp. There are at least fifty people, as John claimed. The smoke I saw comes from fires burned to generate energy in what looks like kilns. And he also has solar panels. Lots of them. I wonder if that's the twinkling I saw from so far away.

Shacks are placed in circles, around the center area. John's house is the biggest one in the middle. Our building is next to his. Outside the shacks is a wall made of large industrial baskets filled with sand. There are guard towers interposed around the compound. Rifles stick out the top like cigarettes. The whole place smells like sewage and dirt.

The people of John's group are all dirty and covered with what I now take to be soot. I imagine it's from working the kilns. They all seem friendly. To me. And the family, but I see MacGee receive evil eyes, and someone even bumped him aside. I guess news travels fast here. Though I'm sad to leave the comfort of our previous area, I'm happy to be in a place that I would dare call civilized. The place is nestled by hills to the south.

At night everyone gathers around the center. It is at this point that the lights flicker on. The place has lighting! My insides warm. I am not certain why. Perhaps it's the fact that this was something that I always took for granted, and after having it taken away, having it returned is like seeing an old friend, something familiar from the past life, stroking whichever neurons inside my brain that attend to these matters.

John introduces us all, then turns to me. "Get some sleep. It has been a long trip. I'll give you a tour tomorrow."

I thank him and all five of us return to the hut that has been assigned to us. I am not so tired that I don't notice that there are a few men placed within sight of the door, which has a light above it. Inside, I realize that there are no windows, and the walls of this shack, unlike the corrugated steel and mud mix I've seen on the other shacks, is made entirely of mud and rock. I don't say anything.

"Well, chosen one," MacGee says, with a veneer of sarcasm. "How may we help you?"

We're inside, and though there's enough chatter outside to mask our speech, and though the walls seem thick enough to muffle words, I'm not sure it's wise to start an argument here. MacGee's attitude also hurts me. He's a friend. And I did save him, didn't I?

The family looks at the both of us.

"You two calm down," James says, with a surprising amount of force.

"Good job, Tom," Samantha says as she brushes by me with her breasts to grab a stack of blankets on the floor.

Her touch knocks the tension with MacGee away, and I think about how to see her alone again.

MacGee's looking at me. He shakes his head. I check to make sure James didn't see anything; he seems to be attending to Sarah's needs.

I sit down on the ground, it's a hard clay. I beckon MacGee to sit next to me. The family is now busy setting up their part of the room. They seem excited, even happy that we've come here.

MacGee hesitates, then sits next to me.

"What's wrong?" I whisper. I remember how we talked only a few nights ago. It'd torn down so many walls between us, and given me a chance to lighten the stress in my head. I'll be sad to see walls being erected between us. I can see why he is angry, but we're going to start the forward march of building up the society we always wanted.

He stares at me, lets out air, and with one hand massages his temples. He looks a lot older than he actually is; looks like he's aged in the trip over.

"Are you angry at me? Why? I made sure they didn't touch you. We're friends, remember?"

"That's right," he says, "you did." He pauses as he looks at the family. "You did, thanks."

He says the last part like he's trying to make himself believe his words, rather than directing anything at me.

"You're welcome. And I do consider you a friend, you know that?"

"I do," he replies.

I pause. The air between us is not the same as when we talked that night, when I admitted to him what had happened in my past. Was it those words that affected his mannerism today? No, it couldn't have been. He was the only one willing to put up with my olfactory senses the other day. Even when it sounded crazy, he'd backed me. That has to be worth something, right? I want that back, the times when the air between us is not fused with the possibility of rejection, a hint of violence, but is filled with complete acceptance.

"What's going on?" I ask.

"I don't belong here," he says without hesitation.

"Why do you say that?" I ask, though I know he doesn't like the religiosity that is slathered around this place. Every door I saw had a cross—except this shack.

"They've already said I don't belong, and I know they're right."

"Who said that?" I ask, anger bubbling. I like this better: feeling like there's someone to smite, rather

130

than having to dig around inside myself to solve a problem.

MacGee scoffs. "What're you going to do, huh? You may be bigger and stronger and faster, but they outnumber you."

"And they listen to me. John does."

MacGee leans in to whisper: "That's only because he's sizing you up. Remember that. He knows you're smart and quick and strong. That doesn't mean that he likes you, or will let you live if it suits him to see you die."

I nod my head, though I'm not certain about his words. He seems to be speaking above and beyond what I can comprehend. And he sounds much like a man speaking his last wishes. I hope he doesn't continue in this vein because he's depressing me.

"He spoke to me on the trip over here. This, John of yours," MacGee says.

"What did he say?" I ask.

"He asked if I was going to convert, that he had room for people who turned their backs on their evil ways."

"And you agreed?" I ask, hoping that he did. I didn't know why MacGee wouldn't just lie to John.

"I told him I'd think about it."

I look at the family; I catch Samantha staring at me, and I look away. I don't want to deal with her right now.

"What did he say?" I ask.

"He said that I'd better think of something quick or else he'd soon send me on my way to the final judge."

I bit the inside of my mouth. I knew John must've had a mean streak; after all, to survive in this world *I* knew what had to be done. And I hadn't trusted

MacGee when I first saw him, why should I expect someone else to do the same?

"Then what?" I ask.

"Nothing. He was about to leave, and I asked him if he was planning on marrying you," MacGee says and flashes me an ugly smile.

I shook my head. "You didn't... did you?"

"I did. No sense of humor, I tells ya." MacGee pulled up his jacket and showed me his bruise on the side of his ribcage.

"Does it hurt?"

"Of course, I think he wears steel toed boots."

I shake my head and grimace my mouth in a sort of silent apology.

"What he said next is what you should be interested in."

"What's that?"

"He leaned in real close like to whisper and he said: 'you're lucky Tom vouched for you, that'll save you for now. Usually we make sinners like you confess, then send you on your way to the Maker to see if you were lying about the confession.' Then he grabbed my balls and squeezed them. 'One false move out of you and not even your friend will stop what's coming.'"

I think that maybe MacGee's embellishing a little for his own sake. Yet in John's threat I feel a certain pride because it proves that my words hold a certain amount of power, or at least sway, over John.

"There's one more thing, Tom," MacGee says, this time with more fear than before.

"What?"

"I asked him if he hated me so much why didn't he just let me go on my way so I wouldn't pollute his flock."

"What did he say?"

"He said there was no leaving his flock. And his rein was over His Kingdom. If that meant he had to purge every inch of it of heathens like myself, then so be it."

"Oh," I say, and think about what it means. It's not that large of a step from what I thought of John before, though it does mean that MacGee cannot leave.

"You know what that means, right?"

"What?"

"Tom," MacGee says in voice that suddenly gets lower. "It means none of us can leave, that we are all his prisoners. Get it?"

I look up at the family. They're still busy tidying up their side of the shack. How can it take them this long to clean up so little? But that wasn't the point. MacGee has said something that makes perfect sense. We are prisoners. And though I'm certain that I'll be fine, the family too, I am not so certain about MacGee. He can't leave. Will he bend, then?

"Tom?"

I turn back to MacGee.

"You paying attention?"

"I get you. I figured there would be a probation. The world the way it is, that only made sense."

"Yes it would make sense, if that was the only thing that mattered, but we can't leave, you get that?" MacGee says.

"I get it, and yeah, I agree it's not the best policy in the world," I say, and at the same time I wonder if it's that bad of a policy. How had I reacted when I knew Bill and Paul were at large in my area? I definitely didn't feel safe, did I? Perhaps that was the same conclusion that John had come to. He must have seen that letting people go, in a world without many resources, will only send them right back at you. Except this time you won't know where they are. Would I have let MacGee go if he only wanted to move on? I'm not certain.

"Best policy in the world?" MacGee says, louder than the hushed voices we have been using until this point. The family glances over, then goes back to their work. "You know exactly what this means. These are the nuts I was talking about, remember?"

"I remember," I say. Yet I don't want to get into an argument about this, I want to make sure MacGee isn't self-destructive.

"Then how can you be so nonchalant about this?" MacGee asks.

"I just don't think it's that bad."

"You understand his other implication?"

I don't know what MacGee is talking about. Is he jealous that I've found a potential friend? "You mean that he takes what I say seriously, what's wrong with that?"

"There's nothing wrong with that," MacGee says. "What I'm saying is what he does to the people who don't believe the way he wants them to."

"You mean the non-believers," I say, correcting him.

"No, that's not what I mean. Remember these people are nuts."

"They're religious and you don't like religious people," I say, correcting his slight.

"Bullshit, Tom. What would you have called people who were living out in the desert before the bombs fell?"

"Crazy," I reply, though I don't want to.

"Exactly."

"But that's before the bombs fell. Once the nukes started to fly all that went out the window. Now the world as you and I know it is crazy, while the people who were true believers are not."

"No," MacGee says, rolling his eyes.

"Why, because you don't like what they believe? Is that why they're nuts? Then I'm a believer too MacGee, don't you get that?"

"I'm sorry, I didn't mean anything by it," MacGee says quietly.

I fall silent, waiting to hear more. MacGee keeps coming back to the same point, and it always reveals his hatred for Christians. He must know that this isn't the way to live a fruitful life, right? He continues on this path of hate, and he won't have much left of himself. Nevertheless, I am his friend, and I wait for him to say something else.

"What I mean is that," MacGee says while raising his hand to make a cutting motion, "they seek out people and kill them if they don't agree with them."

I can see why this is disturbing, and yet I can also see the need for it. Can't let enemies lurk in the shadows, can we? That'll only lead to possible attacks.

"All right," I say. "But it's a tough world, and we don't know what they've been through."

MacGee stares at me, I can see the energy leaving his body. His body expands and contracts, but it also trembles, and he seems a frightened little bird.

"Okay, listen," he says. "It isn't just about them killing those who aren't Christians. You get that, right?"

"No," I say, measuring up MacGee and wondering what he's going to say next.

"People like this... with this much fervor, always turn on their own. By that I mean other Christians.

You watch, Tom, just watch. You'll see that they'll start picking on people for slight differences, and then it won't matter if they're Christians or not."

I look down on the floor. Again MacGee's train of thought has left me grasping for an answer, because I've no clue what he's getting at. I remind myself that he must be scared and that this is his way of trying to deal with it. That's fine, he can be scared, but he shouldn't make up things like this. I decide to allow him these words.

"Are you going to convert?"

He lets out a short puff of air, angry, and stares at me while shaking his head. "Why should I convert? Who'd believe me anyways?"

Does he want to die? This doesn't make sense; he doesn't believe in an afterlife, so what could he possibly be trying to martyr himself for? "They will. If they're nuts, like you said, they're looking for an excuse to hang you. So don't give it to them. Say you've converted and go on living."

"What sort of life is that? Give up my ideals for these idiots?" MacGee says in a soft growl.

Again I don't understand him, but he's my friend, I remind myself, so I'll try to convince him. Why *is* he being so adamant? There's nothing in the after-life for him, so this should be an easy choice for him. Of course, I believe in heaven and hell, and I want MacGee to live on, not only so I can have a friend, but secretly I think that he's a good man, Christian if you will, and that he stands a chance of making it to heaven, and I also think that barring that, he will sooner or later come to the side of the Lord. I can't tell him this, though, as he won't take it well.

"Are you serious? You're my friend, the only one I have in this new world and you're telling me you're going to leave me because you want to spite some people you don't even care about?" I say.

"And you want me to give up on my ideals?"

I pause, wondering how I can get this wrinkled man in front of me to relent. His pride seems to be the problem. Perhaps what convinced me will convince him.

"Remember what you said about rebuilding the country?" I ask.

"What about it?"

"Well, isn't this the best way to do it? Working with these people. They have the technology, and with that we can build towards a future for a new nation. Right?"

MacGee looks at the ground, tossing his head back and forth just slightly.

"Okay," he says slowly. "But it's not just about technology. That's just a minor matter. The important thing are the ideals behind that nation. And these people do not have that. They're only standing on the shoulders of others. That's what matters."

I think about this. It doesn't sound right, but I've no way of arguing against him. I think of another way to pierce his armor.

"What about what you told me? Is that all bullshit?" I ask, throwing anger into my words.

"What?" he asks.

"The things you said about surviving. That's what you told me, right? That surviving was the most important thing?"

"That's right," he said with a dejected look.

"Then? Why don't you just survive?"

He looks at me. I hold my breath. Am I such a child that I need him? I have John listening to me, and right now John is the most powerful man around.

Why should I worry about what MacGee says? That logic, if that's what it is, doesn't work, and I wait for MacGee to speak.

"All right, Tom. I'll 'convert'," says MacGee as if the choice of dying was so much better.

I want to hug him, but I don't.

"Thanks, we'll work something out, we will," I say. These words aren't backed with thought.

"You really think this will end well, don't you?" MacGee asks.

"Of course, why wouldn't it?"

He shakes his head. Sad. "All you've been through and you think it'll end well?"

I look at him, his wrinkles now like contour lines on a map. He's very old, I assumed wise. "What do you mean? You think they won't believe you?"

"No, I think they will. But sooner or later what I said about their ideals not being in the right place will bite us all, even you, oh chosen one."

We go to sleep that night, me sleeping on one end, and Samantha on the other.

I have my doubts about MacGee's words, and as I drift to sleep I'm sure that MacGee is only worried about what'll happen to himself. I'll keep an eye out for what he mentioned, but I'm sure that he's being paranoid. It could be that this close to the end of his life he doesn't want everything he's done to be for naught; so he must be clinging to ideas that he held on to for most his life; doing otherwise would erase his entire history, and who can live with that?

The next morning they serve us breakfast. It's an amazing stew, with eggs on the side. Yes real eggs. I look at MacGee when I taste them. His lips have a piece of egg on them. He smiles.

"This must be the best food I've had in years," he says.

"I know," I say, with my mouth open.

"Me too," Sarah says with a bright look on her face. I look at Samantha and smile; she smiles back. It isn't tinged with lust; it's merely friendly. I like this. A lot. As the food settles in my stomach, I know now what I have to do. I won't fall victim to my desires anymore. I will work towards that goal, of building something, of fending for the human race.

A man, one I saw hanging around John, steps in.

"How's the food?" he asks.

"Fan-fucking-tastic," MacGee says, spitting out some food when he speaks.

Sarah giggles, but shuts up when her parents snap their heads and eyes at her.

The man sizes up MacGee and thinks to say something.

"It's great, thanks a lot," I say, hoping to avoid confrontation. I'm not trying to kiss ass, but I want to give a good impression. Also I'm trying to see how the man will react.

The man looks at me, and I can see his demeanor soften up. "That's good to hear."

"You guys eat this everyday?" I ask.

"That's right. It comes from our farm and livestock," the man says, standing taller.

"Livestock?" James asks.

I am impressed. I get up and put out my hand. "I'm Tom, have we met yet?"

"I'm Zeb," he says and shakes my hand. "Pleased to meet you."

The tension in the air evaporates.

"John wants to see everyone in a few minutes," Zeb says, and looking at me adds: "If that's all right."

"Of course," I say. "We'll get ready."

As we prepare ourselves, brush our teeth, and tidy up, I look at the clay floor and I notice a yellow powdery substance that's patterned in odd gothic patterns. I point it out to MacGee.

"Some sort of art?" I ask.

"No. That's dried up blood," and when he says this he gives me a look like there is something we both know, though I'm not certain what this is.

A few minutes later we're standing in the large meet house. It's a large single roomed building. It feels like a courthouse, mixed with elements of a church. I'm not sure what its purpose is, but I don't feel good about it.

At one end is a large table. John sits in the middle with three people on either side of him. Lining the walls are a few men with weapons on them. I remember I have a handgun hidden in my pants, but I decide not to touch it since it'll give away the one layer of protection I have.

For some reason I think none of these people will like it if I'm armed. The roof of the place is also clay, reinforced with steel beams; everything smells like a clean horse farm. I can only imagine that they bought the beams from before the nuclear war. The windows are large mouths with what looks like dirty plastic covering them.

I examine the men. They're definitely surrounding us, and they all look grim. We are led to the table by Zeb, and as we do the men slowly close in on us. My stomach knots up.

Easy, no need to inflict harm just yet.

"Nice place, John," I say with a smile.

The people to either side of John all shoot me hostility with their glares, and one starts to say something, but John raises his hand.

"Thank you Tom," he says and looks at the people to either side of him. "This is Tom. He's a believer, and he'll do well by us." He finishes speaking and looks at me with something like concern. "We built this, everything you see with our own hands. We create, and we do it for the Lord. Soon you'll do the same."

His voice, his words, fill the building. My take of his words, however, is that they're laced with condescension, especially the last part. I'll keep mum for now. I'll not, however, go around taking orders. "I don't doubt that," I say.

"I welcome all of you," John says, "and I hope that we will continue with all of you helping the cause of rebuilding His Kingdom."

The place is perfectly made for John's voice. I can feel his voice pushing through my chest, echoing off the walls and vibrating my head. I remember to keep an eye on the men around us. They haven't moved. I take in MacGee, who's next to me and the family who are next to him.

"James," John says.

"Yes... sir," James says.

"This is your family?"

"It is."

"What was your work before the fall?" John asks.

"I was a geologist, sir," James says again, stumbling over his fricatives like he's scared of them.

I see that John, and the men to either side of him, like James' fear. In fact, they seem to eat it up, smiling to each other each time James stumbles. Even though this reminds me of the men who tried to kill me after the Fall, I push it aside.

"Doing what?"

"I was looking for proof to show that the world is indeed as old as the Bible says it is."

They like it.

"So you've been doing the Lord's work for some time then?"

"All my life, sir."

"Well, I'm sure you'll be able to help us. You *are* willing to help us?"

"I am, sir. I will."

I take my eyes off James because I'm disgusted with how much he's groveling. MacGee, on the other hand is staring down John, and I can see that he's seething. I hope he'll have enough of a mind to say the right thing. I want him to live. Even though I like the words John has thrown my way, I know that we can't be friends. MacGee might be the only friend I have.

"Do you know anything about mining?" John asks.

"Yes, I do. That was my previous job," James replies.

"Good," John says. "You can tell where to mine for minerals?"

"Yes, most minerals, gold, and oil."

The men around John all break out into smiles.

"Very well. Give us a moment to convene," John says then turns to the men to either side. They all pass him a coin. He looks at them and smiles.

"Well, to show that you are a true believer, and that you are willing to work for the Lord you must kneel," John says, and stands up.

"Yes," James says quickly.

John puts out his hand.

I squeeze my eyes shut and look at my hands to make sure that this is really happening. Where are we? Is this a fiefdom?

James kneels and looks up as John thrusts his hand out. "Are you a loyal subject?"

"Yes," James says, looking at the hand as if even he, so willing to grovel, couldn't believe this is happening. James looks back at me for a second.

"Kiss the ring," John says.

James takes John's hand and after looking at it for another second, kisses it.

I step forward slightly to steady myself. This *is* happening. I can see that every one of John's men are looking on as if this is expected of everyone that they see, or absorbed into this flock.

Yet the silliness of the act only makes it that much more sinister, and I start to sweat. It may have been silly, but they look ready to kill anyone who would dare not do so. That fact, that something silly could be made so serious, hits me hard and I inhale deep breaths so that I don't get woozy.

"Zeb, will you be so kind as to take the family to their new place of residence? By the kiln on the North side." John turns his eyes to James. "I think you will find the place, and your neighbors quite to your liking."

"I'm sure we will," James says, gives a half bow and is led off, Samantha taking his hand, and Sarah scuttling behind them.

The door closes behind the family.

"And you Tom?" John asks.

"What about me?"

John pauses for a second. I can tell he doesn't like it when I talk like this. "I worked on computers."

"Software or hardware?" John asks.

"Both, though mainly software towards the end."

"Any language?"

"Mostly python, but I can learn any other one."

"Good, we'll be able to use that."

I don't like the idea of being used for anything. But if I lash out now to save my pride, I will jeopardize MacGee's chances of surviving.

"I'm glad," I say, my voice stretching as the lie leaves my lips. "I will help out in any way possible."

The men around John nod, though no coins are passed around.

"I know you will, Tom," says John. "We don't have to convene about you. We will give you a place in the North as well."

"Sounds good." I say. My chest tightens as I know what I have to do. Remember MacGee, I think, push that pride aside.

John stands up. "So do you kneel to the Kingdom?"

"Yes," I say as I step forward.

I glance around to see if everyone is going to break out into a smile. They don't.

Am I going to do this? I have to, I remind myself, MacGee's life depends on it. Yet it seems so outlandish. I've only read about this in books about ancient times. Or fairy tales.

I draw in a deep breath. This *is* a fairy tale; everything about this life, when compared to the previous one, seems like a horrid story. Do it, I say, as I see John's head tilt in confusion. What does it mean to kneel? It's only a simple movement; you kneel to pick up things off the ground, so why would it matter here? I've even kissed women's hands. So why would kissing his ring matter?

I kneel, look up and kiss the hand. John nods, a smirk on his face.

I get up. It means nothing I tell myself. But it does, oh it means everything. I feel myself turning submissive to John, to the others. Of course, this is why humans were forced to do this in the past. I'm not sure if it's the specific act, or that any gesture, if labeled as submissive and treated as such would always be just that. I stare at the ground trying to find my manhood.

"Very well, you may leave," John says.

The words echo in the distance. I can see everyone visibly lean into MacGee like lions waiting for the kill. I'm nervous that he'll be killed. I slowly build up the power inside me to speak. The memory of MacGee backing me about the smell helps.

"If I may, I'd like to stay. He is a friend of mine," I say, and when the faces don't seem to consider me, I continue: "A good friend."

A guard next to me steps up and pulls a knife. "John said to leave," he says moving the knife towards me. The man has a large frame, wider than mine, but though his face is young, pockmarks give him an aged look. His flesh is like an old man's, it hangs delicately, and he moves slowly. I pause, the submissiveness I experienced before makes me loathe to move, but I can't let anyone just push me around; I know what begging does to another man's soul: it only makes him want to eat it.

I grab the man's wrist, and pull out the knife from his grasp and turn it on his neck. I can see from the way everyone freezes that they don't expect this. I also know to look at John to make sure he's not taking this the wrong way. His face seems to be regarding me with mild curiosity.

"Don't point a knife at your brother," I manage to say to the man, and loud enough that others can hear me. I throw the knife to the floor and bow my head to John. I know that it's his word that matters. "Sorry about that John, but I found that disrespectful."

I can hear the men to either side of him mumbling unkind words. A man to the left of John pulls at his sleeve, and John leans over and hears him out.

John shakes his head. "Brothers," he says as he stands up. "We cannot go pulling knives on one another. And Tom is one of us now."

Everyone agrees. I relax.

"You may stay Tom."

"Thank you," I say and half bow my head.

"MacGee," John says, his voice picking up its boom, and he sits back down. "Are you ready to convert?"

MacGee glances about, he knows he's on thin ice, but I can see him fighting with the small part of him that doesn't want to ever bow to men like these. "I do... sir."

"You renounce all your previous ways? Your vile and evil ways of a non-believer?"

"Yes, I do."

"Do you accept the Lord as your savior?"

"I do." MacGee slightly bows his head, and I'm sure that everyone around believes him. I know I do.

"What did you do before this?"

"I was a prospector, looking for minerals and such. Before that I was a scientist, data crunching, mainly."

"Statistics are the reason we're here today," says the man to the left of John, and everyone nods their heads in unison.

"That's right," another man pipes up. "They're the way that non-believers turned people away from the Lord.

Another approving hum goes up in the hall.

John raises his hand. "No, using it the wrong way can get you in trouble. If we control it, though, it won't be used in that manner."

"I disagree," a man to the right of John says.

This disagreement strikes me as odd. No one seems to react. Perhaps things are not as they appear.

"Why?" John asks.

"The sciences were used to break down tradition, one by one. No matter how hard we try there'll be no way to turn the tide once the gate is open. And in addition the gatekeeper will be a non-believer? Or a person who was once that? *This* is trouble."

John nods his head, as if he was going to change his mind.

"MacGee," John says. "What do you have to say about this?"

"That there are many uses for statistics," MacGee replies.

I can hear the tension in his voice. Even he is searching for some patience to explain the importance of his job to people he hated and most likely were his intellectual inferiors.

"I think, when you're referring to tradition, you mean the social sciences. I have never dealt with that.

But I have dealt with it in engineering and the like. It has its uses, and especially for building."

Another moment of chatter arises from the men on either side of John.

"He has a sharp tongue, this non-believer," another man says. "I don't believe him."

John nods his head.

"What do you have to say to that?" the man who voiced the accusation asks.

"That I'm lying?" MacGee asks.

"See?" the man says.

John raises his hand, something I'm glad for because if the man's going to turn this into a schoolyard bullying session, I'm going to lose my cool.

"Listen, brothers," John says. "We must be careful not to lose sight of the fact that he has converted. Under the Lord's eyes. Let us give him a chance. If we see he's a tool for the devil, then we shall deal with him accordingly."

The men nod their heads as if John's words are enough to erase their doubts.

"Do you agree then to work for the Lord from now on?" John asks, his voice booming again.

"I do, sir," MacGee says.

"We will watch you carefully, and if you choose to do anything that is out of place, we shall deal with you swiftly. Do you understand?"

"I do; I will not disappoint," MacGee replies.

"Very well," John says and the ceremony continues. MacGee kneels and kisses the hand. John then sends him away. When I'm about to follow him, John calls out my name.

"Yes?" I ask. I can feel the guard, from whom I grabbed the knife, staring a hole into the side of my face. His look is not friendly, and some of the other guards share his anger. I will have to watch my step.

"Will you come with me? I have a few things I want to discuss with you in person."

John places his hand around my shoulder and takes me back to his house, which is attached to this great hall or courtroom. I'm glad that we'll be away from the eyes of the others.

A guard follows behind us, and John turns to him. "No need to come, I want to be alone with *brother* Tom." The guard scuttles away.

As we enter his house I brush the handle of my gun. The first room we enter is a large room, cement walls, no windows, maps and charts strewn across the vertical axis, and a large table in the middle with chairs around it. It smells like a stuffy place where the sweat of too many angry men has stewed without the air to breath it out.

John shuts the door behind me and locks it. As soon as he does, his shoulders sag slightly.

"This is your house?" I ask.

"Well, it's my house as well as being our planning room. It allows me to come up with ideas before anyone else," John says, with a soft grin on his face, something I've not seen before.

He has been hiding his true self to the others. I find myself drawn to him.

"Tell me, Tom, what do you think of this compound of ours?"

This is either a treacherous question or something that will be a harbinger of our friendship to come. "I find it very inspiring," I say, a half-truth that I hope will suffice for now.

He laughs. "Come on Tom, you're not near the others," he says and looks at me with a sad face. He waits a few more seconds before he realizes that I'm not going to answer.

"Are you losing your fighting spirit Tom?" He smiles.

I glance back at the door, it's definitely secure, and I can't hear anything. Why do I feel like everyone in the compound's watching us?

"Do you do this often?" I ask.

"Do what?"

"This."

"It's usually women." John flashes a smile that I find hideous. "Why?"

"Because we're getting a lot of looks from your... flock," I say the last word with added emphasis, and I immediately regret it because I can see the seriousness travel through his face. I need to be very careful with John.

"They're not used to seeing someone come in here alone after just being accepted into our flock," John says.

Silence falls between us, and I hear nothing but distant tinks; the precious move forward that other people working sounds like. I haven't heard something like this since the fall. I wonder if it's something I've missed. I felt more natural—a state I would only call one that seemed more basic, or a way that allowed me to dig deep, not into my thoughts but into my instincts—in the state before: the quiet of the cave, of Jenny's presence, of family and MacGee in my periphery.

With this hum of human activity that I'm now surrounded by, I feel a flutter of my heart, not something that's good, just a push, a jolt, as if I'll have to run with the herd, or be trampled, and this scares me out of my wits. I'm back with humanity. And what of those moments before? Those times where I was certainly a human being, but didn't act in a prescribed manner—in a civilized manner.

Please... The breathing of the man, the glint in his eye. Did I see that? Or is my mind now taking patches from elsewhere so that the picture appears more complete? Why does my mind do that? To torment me? *Don't...* The breathing of the man, the hopelessness with which he spoke his last words. And what was he talking about? Himself? Did he want a reprieve? To live one more day? Forgiveness? I gave him none of that. And if he wanted Jenny to be left untouched I gave him none of that either. I had erased an entire family from the world.

Me.

That was what I had been. It's the past now and I should be willing to step forward and forget. This hum of humanity, almost like a city, like those beacons of shining light on hills or swamps of the past, is now my future. Forgiveness. The Lord has obviously given it to me; I should take it without hesitation.

"Tom," John says, waving his hand across my field of vision. "You with me?"

I come back to the room, the man's words, *Please... Don't...* still linger, not as a sound but as a vision, and a feeling. Of hope?

"Yeah?" I say, again uncertain about being in this room with John.

"Take a look at this," he says as he sweeps his hand over the table. I walk over to it to see that it's a map under a glass surface marked with various colors. I see X's and dotted lines and solid lines and skulls. I see a faint star over a few squares and notice the contour lines of hills next to it.

"That us?" I ask.

"It is," he says, with an approving smile.

I look over the map again; I can feel John's eyes washing over my face.

"You're smart Tom."

I graze his face with my eyes, then the wall behind him.

"You may be a little rough on the edges, but I assume that's just your way of being. Probably had to do some crazy things to get to where you are, right?"

I'm careful not to nod my head, nor to disagree with him. He knows the story of the cave. It makes me one of the chosen ones in his eyes, or at least he said so. But there are also the stories that follow that one. I can't divulge that right now, can I? The tinking sound continues... *Please... Don't.* The world moving forward. That's what I did, isn't it? *Please... Don't...*

She jumps.

"Tom?"

John looks concerned.

"We all have our journeys, don't we?" I say, hoping that the cliché will keep him away from my blank stares for now. I notice, in this room of stale male odors, that John smells exceptionally clean, like he's stepped out of a bath of flowers. I wonder if he has a shower. We made do without showers for so long that I start to realize that a lot of the male body odor is coming from me.

"We do," John says.

I look at my feet for a second and notice a splash of yellow on the ground, a clay floor that seems to have absorbed most of the color. Blood. MacGee said.

"I can trust you, can't I?" John asks.

"You can."

"I hope so... You're right. I don't bring many people here. In fact, though we have a council, they're mostly idiots. I rarely take them in for anything more than berating them, or correcting their moral compass."

The blood on the floor still infects my mind. I don't like that I'm standing on old blood, but I have my demons. Why shouldn't I allow him to have his? His voice sounds honest enough, and if I can become his friend this would be the start of a new beginning for me. Perhaps I needed him as much as he needed me. "And you're bringing me here to test me," I say.

"Like I said I don't let just anyone here to talk to them. To have a conversation."

Again I hear the hint of threat in his voice, as if there isn't a thing in the world that he sees as equal. I hold off on snapping back. Flattery, that's what he's after. "Of course, and I appreciate it. So what do you want to talk about? The weather?" I smile after the last comment.

John smiles back.

"What I said before," I say. "I meant it."

"Which part? When you had a knife to one of my men's neck?"

I chuckle. John joins. I like him a little more, and can see why he was picked as a leader.

"No," I reply. "The part where I said I wanted to help build a new beginning. A new nation. America. But this time it'll be done the right way."

"I believe you. We can definitely build towards something new."

"We will become the beacon of civilization, and I want to help that along," I say.

When his pause grows, I bide my time by looking at the map. Did I say the wrong thing?

"I concur."

"Be the good in this world," I say.

"Well, that will be the goal. Right?"

This I don't like, but I remember what I too have done and thought. Forgiveness. If I want it I should give it out more often. The Lord is kind.

"That should be the goal," I agree.

The tinking continues. Part of me wonders about making the same mistakes as before.

"I'll be honest. I'm the leader here. But I need someone to rule with who will be someone I can trust."

"Fair enough," I say, thinking on an appropriate answer. "And I'm willing to be that person," I say.

"Very well. Do you agree that in the fight for good we must sometimes do things that we don't agree with?"

Another knee jerk reaction rises against his words, but I fight it. This seems like a way to bury those horrid things in my past. "I agree."

John nods his head, smiles at the map.

"You see this map?" he asks.

"Right, it's of our general area." I make out the path we've traveled to get here. I make out the tight contour lines of the cliff face I climbed. For a moment I feel the wind in my face, the thrill of climbing on and on, reaching the top and feeling like the only man on an island in the sky.

In the background the hum of digging continues.

"That's right," John says, leaning over the map like some great general. I feel like I did right before I had to bow. John made me do that. I try to forget, as this makes me mad, but I only switch over to thinking how John looks like he's playing at how to be a general, and not one at all. This is his dream come true, the end of the earth. And he wants to play at everything he was never allowed to before the nukes fell. That makes me feel even more like when I was bowing: that this is a fantastical land. I lose some respect for John and further dismiss the bowing incident.

"We send a group out in a different direction each day. They come back to tell us what we've found. Sometimes we tell them to go out for a week. That has been the furthest they've gone so far."

"Exploring the area," I say."

"That's right," John replies.

"You were looking for other people. That's how you found us."

"Exactly." John leans over the map, his legs stretching; he's balancing on his toes. I see him doing this as a child.

"Have you explored everything on this map?" I ask as I make a mental note of where the cave should be. Though I want to hide it from him, I know it'll be a sign of my good faith if I tell him where it is. Then I think of the bodies. Will they find them? And what will they make of it then? Surely I'll be able to wash my hands, after all what forensics team will there be? As I think this I realize that my hands are getting wet: they'll see my guilt the moment they bring up the bodies. Maybe not for some of them. But when Bill or Jenny's body gets pulled up I'll twitch. I'll remember. I chew the inside of my mouth so that I don't daze off into a land where John will have to snap me out again.

"We have, for the most part. There are places that we didn't expect to find anything, but, as with you and your group, people will live just about anywhere."

"You've found others?"

"We have," John says with a sigh.

"They're here?"

"We've searched for at least a fifty miles in every direction." He raises his hand as he speaks, "Not that it means we have found everything to be found, but we have the basic overlay of *our* area."

John takes the map and pulls it out from under the glass. It has a cardboard backing that slides out, underneath the table in a slotted tray. He pulls out another map. This one is detailed too, but much bigger. No state lines, it's purely a topographical map. I see hints of blue to the west with the Pacific marked. There's a faint red contour on the map that I imagine marks us at the center. I try to make out where it would be. Oregon or Nevada or Utah. Funny how hard it is to tell without the state lines marked.

I like that they've set about a concrete way of finding others, and, I imagine, slowly expanding the population. It'll be a great way to include others. MacGee's warning hits me; they tortured and killed those who didn't agree.

Never judge.

"How did you find us, if we were hidden, and you assumed you searched the area?"

"Luck. Someone decided to cut across that hill you were nestled in and smelled your lot. They observed you for a few hours before heading back for support."

I try not to betray the fact that I want to know what they observed. Did they see me and Samantha? I think I smelled them once when I was with her.

"That *is* luck," I manage to say.

"And you want to know if we've found others?" John asks.

"Well?"

"We have. We've found plenty of others." He points to the map as he says this. "See?"

I look, but I don't see what he means. This map has fewer marks than the previous one. I'm also surprised to hear him say that he found lots of people.

"The black spots marks where we have seen others, but not approached them," John says.

"Why not?" I ask.

"Because they're too large or well armed for us to take on."

"Could you approach them and see if they're friendly?" I notice only three black marks. If what MacGee said was right and the people who survived were the crazy survivalists, then only further disaster loomed. But what if they were good? "What if they're Christians?" I ask.

"Maybe," John replies; the look on his face says that he considers my reply to be foolish.

"So only three that you've seen and not approached, right?"

"The others..." John says, as if it's something he didn't want to talk about. "Well we absorbed a few. A few believers..."

Again the hesitation. Wouldn't I hesitate too? Wisdom to know the difference. I remember this and gently nudge him to speak by staying silent and eager.

The hum in the background continues. I realize that I'm not certain what it was they are building, or digging to.

"How many did you absorb?" I ask, realizing that he won't speak on his own.

"A handful, maybe three or so."

"How many others did you find?"

"A lot. In pairs, or groups. Men and women, sometimes children..."

My stomach churns at that thought. He harmed children? And if so, so what? Was it that bad? Why?

And why did it matter? How old were those young men, or perhaps old boys that I killed? Those sons.

"I can see from your face that you do not approve," John says.

"Don't assume that, John. I'm merely taking in what you're saying. I am definitely not judging."

"Very well. I'm sure you've talked to MacGee."

"Like I said, he's a friend of mine," I reply. John's tone switches from meek to stolid in the past few sentences.

"Did he tell you what we did with non-believers?"

"Yes, he said you asked them to convert, and if they didn't they would be killed."

"And what do you think about this?"

John's face has turned into a frozen sea, a mask that is boring a hole through me. I take note of this change. He's able to twist and turn his emotions to his own uses. Just when I thought I was going to be able to twist him for information, he turns the blade on me.

What do I think? Do I even know what I think? And more importantly, what should I say?

"Does it matter what I think?"

"It does," John replies.

I feel a tension in my heart. "Perhaps you could give me more details. But it's my belief that if people aren't willing to at least convert, or try to work for the furthering humanity's cause, then you cannot..." I pause, weighing my words, he will remember what I said here in this room and I have to be careful to say something that has substance, but will not weigh down my choices in the future. "Trust them to be on their own. There isn't much out there, and if you leave enemies there, they will come after you."

John closes his eyes as if my words are a wind.

I wait.

The tinking sound continues. No matter how tense it is in here, I don't feel much like leaving the room. I know as soon as we're out there with the others around, John will change, because he's too smart not to change, and to be as open as he is in front of me. Whether that's good or not is beyond me.

I smell something like body odor coming off John and it calms me to know that he can be dragged through the dirt like the rest of us.

"So you agree that it's important to have true believers as we rebuild. Right? And that sometimes we have to make hard choices?" John asks and opens his eyes.

"Yes... I do," I say.

"Because you shouldn't look upon us like we're marauding bands out there to kill anyone not to our liking. That was, is not our intention. We *are* the way forward and for anyone we met if they chose not to go with us, they were choosing a worse fate, for certain," John says.

I want to say something, but John continues before I can speak.

"And I'll tell you what we found." He traces his hand on the glass surface above the map as he speaks. "We found an entire family murdered for their food. Mother father and son shot just like that," John says and shakes his head.

I'm glad I stayed quiet because I am sure that the place his finger hovers over is the same place where the family attacked me. Do I have a defense? With no other witnesses what he says sounds like the truth, perhaps it is. "Really?" I say, my voice almost cracking with the dichotomous strain in my head.

"That's right. And let me ask you this," John says and stretches out his forefinger, a long bony extension that's almost as long as my face. "Which is better, to die for lowly scraps by some heathen who will only continue to scrape by, or to die for an ideal... for God?" He raises his finger to the sky, and his voice picks up that boom quality that he seems to save for points he wants to make. In this small, enclosed room, I feel his voice tickle my tongue and shake my veins.

How am I to answer that? There seems like there should be more nuance to a statement about killing, but I also am not about to take the side of a heathen killing people for scraps, lest John figures out it was me doing that killing. In a way, his rationale is not so outlandish. Was not an ideal something to die for, while material goods were not?

"I'd assume the latter," I say.

"Exactly," John replies. "Is not the man who kills for scraps merely an animal, while the man who kills for his Lord, for an ideal that will do more for him, and his fellow men than food, that will spiritually satisfy him, is that not what we should die for? Are we not doing the Lord's work, and if so, how can anyone ever think we're doing something evil?"

I shrug; John's point of view seems to make sense, though he is acting fervent.

"Do you agree?" John asks, and he closes his eyes again.

"I do," I say. Not because I feel that I have to, or because of my guilt, but because somewhere in this song and dance I feel that there has been some truth, that an ideal is something better and something we can work towards, and in this righteous speech I know I will find my forgiveness, or my cocoon from which I can emerge anew.

"Good." John opens his eyes when he says this, like he was waiting for that answer to come back to this world. "Let me tell you a little more about our operations."

He tells me about their greenhouse gardens, the mining that allows them to gather some metals and build a few bits of machinery, the solar panels and mirrors. Their compound spent millions of dollars in the past decade finding this place and securing it from the prying eyes of the federal government. Finally he brings up one problem:

"When I said only a few people have been absorbed, I say that with a heavy heart."

"Why's that?" I ask.

"We have a breeding problem right now."

"What do you mean? I saw women..."

"No, none of them pregnant, not since the fall. We have a few doctors who say that it's from the radiation."

"The mines didn't help?"

"Well, when it happened, we weren't completely prepared. But the mine still has an open face. It wasn't sealed properly. So we had no choice but to be exposed. Though we had it better than a lot of other exposure victims."

"From your compound?"

"A few from here. We had to watch them die because there was no saving them. Others had their eyes burned out, clawing and trying to find help." John swallows. "There were scores of them. And we couldn't help them."

"That can't be helped," I say.

"It may not be," he says, his head bowing as if the weight of memories is forcing his body down to the ground. I know what this feels like. I stay quiet. The tinking comes back to life.

Nelson Lowhim

"And of all the other survivors?" I ask, speaking of the pregnancies now.

"Of the remaining ones, we came to the same problem," John says.

"You don't think that there will be any pregnancies?"

"There haven't been any, and we've made sure to tell people that they need to go forth and be plentiful."

I suppress a smirk because I imagine all the grim people trying to procreate every night, not from passion but from a duty to their leader, their God. I brush away the thought because I don't want the Lord to believe that I'm crude—and here in this house I feel especially watched by Him.

"I'm sure that they have," I manage to say. "Perhaps there needs to be some time, between now and the, the fall, for the women to get over their trauma. I'm sure the mind knows to keep the body in check during such times."

John agrees with his face and a slow nod, as if he's looking for something else from me, but he's not going to tell me what.

"Make sense?" I ask.

"It does."

The tinking noise in the background stops, and I hear nothing but the sound of my own blood rushing up to my neck, my stomach rumbles. There will be more between John and I, and I think he knows this too.

"Let's go eat lunch," John says, and I see the tension leave his face.

We eat lunch in the same room as the trials had been conducted. Tables are pulled out and everyone eats at once. I sit next to John, and can see MacGee several tables over, with his head down. No one talks

162

to him; they avoid him like he has a disease. I don't like this, it almost feels like high school where people were randomly chosen for 'x' difference so that others could inflict pain on them, but I remember that such things didn't really change in life, they only morphed. It's best not to stir the social brew for now. I decide to talk to him some other time.

The rest of the day I'm by John's side looking over the mining and the plant projects. The manufacturing that they want to start hasn't gotten into full swing, but it looks amazing. After assuming that the entire world was reduced to rubble and assuming that we would have to live off the scraps that we saved from the past, I'm pleased with what I see. Inside all the gnawing doubts about myself, my past, and hence John and these people, dissipates and I feel more and more a part of them, as well as wanting to help, in any way I can.

Finally, John takes me to their computer room, which is a dusty mess.

"We tried to get our systems back up," John says, "but no one really knew what to do. The one computer engineer we had his eyes scorched when he stared at one of the flashes. His mind was a mess by the time we found him."

"Wandering in the desert?" I ask.

"Yeah, mumbling something about how this was not the way. He recognized our voices... Told us that he had indeed seen the light, that he had talked to God in the past few days and that what we were doing didn't matter. That we were on the wrong path no matter what we did or believed," John says, his face freezing again into a mask of thought.

"Then what?"

163

"We had to put him down. Can't have someone spouting such nonsense, it might get people thinking, you know?"

"Of course."

"It was the only thing we could do," John says, as if he's trying to convince himself rather than me.

I notice that one wall of this room, located near the mines, is a side of the hill. Stacked up are coils after coils of wire.

"Those are fiber optic cables. We were going to wire this whole place up with computers, but we lost a lot of our population, so we decided to wait," John says, his mouth's edges curling into a smile. "We have a small cave entrance, there," he points. "And more cable. We bought about two hundred fifty miles worth of the stuff."

The number seems implausible. I'm impressed. "You were planning on rewiring the entire west coast?" I ask.

"That's right."

"But for now you'll settle for this compound."

"I'll give you men, tell them where to dig, fix these computers and the first thing I want wired are the guard towers and the head quarters."

"Your place," I say.

"That's right, my place. And the main hall. That way people can stay abreast of what's happening with the compound's security."

"What about people's homes?" I ask.

"No," John says without even thinking about it for a moment.

"Why not?"

"I believe that the problems of our previous nation was that people had too many gadgets," John says. "We're keeping away from that."

"Fine," I say and wonder if that's a wise choice. For now it won't matter as the compound is small, but the need to be in touch doesn't seem like it'll go away anytime soon.

"Another thing about the computers," John says.

"Yes?"

"No games on them. I want all games disabled on them."

"Why's that?"

He looks at me funny and shakes his head.

John then leads me to the garage, another hole in the side of the hill. There are dune buggies, dirt bikes, three wheelers, and a couple massive trucks. All of them look like they've been dressed up for effect. A few even have guns at the top.

"Do you have fuel?" I ask.

"Yes, we have a few thousand gallons. But that's it. We need to set up a refinery, but we haven't had luck finding a good source for oil."

"You've been heading out on foot when you could've driven out?"

"It's not as crazy as you think," John says. "Using these, in a landscape so quiet, would automatically take away any element of surprise."

I stare at the truck. When was the last time I'd driven? Something that was once so natural now seemed foreign, and I wanted to climb in and drive.

"And until we find a good way of making more fuel we can't waste what we have. These," John adds, "are all diesel engines."

I don't know what that means.

We tour some more places and before dinner John decides to head off and check the mines. I walk around the compound looking at the people going about their daily chores. It feels so good to be amongst these people.

The tinking sound that emanates from the mine hardly registers. I smell soap; I smell human odors. I even see a few women. My cock twitches, but I push it down with my mind, trying to absorb the place. I want to find MacGee so that I can talk to him. It pains me to see him suffer so much. He, of all people should be glad to be here. It is the epitome of a technological oasis.

As I walk, children run up to me like I'm a foreign man in these parts. A few beautiful girls, barely women, barely bursting on two sides, walk by me with smiles that seem to shake the entire compound's religious ethos into ether. I cannot fathom how no one has been impregnated yet. One thing I notice is that everyone is blonde and blue eyed. The women especially.

I smile at another girl who walks by me with food in her arms. She smells like roses. The smell of the compound, of soap, mud and water, overwhelms the girl's ghost. I try to find where James and his family would be, hoping that it'll lead me to MacGee.

"Tom." I turn when I hear her voice, it's not laced with any desire, and when I look at her I don't feel much desire either. People mill around us.

"Samantha," I say and walk up to her.

She invites me to their new house. It's two rooms: a living room kitchen and a bedroom in the back.

"Where's Sarah?" I ask. The inside is lit with naked electric light bulbs and Christmas lights. With the mud walls, I feel like I'm in Mexico.

"There's school here for the kids. She's out learning and playing. Great, isn't it?"

I nod. "It's an amazing place."

I feel Samantha's hand on mine. Is this what I want? She seems so serene, so happy, why risk this? I look up and know that I will risk it too. I'm looking at her curves and the same rush that used to run through my arteries, and to my cock, is not there. Of course, I'm getting hard, but this time it's because of something else, the familiar smell of hers, her smile, and the way she's twisting under my glare. Though all these things are familiar, there is something different in the combination of it all. This, if we are to interlock our pubic areas, will not be the same as it was before.

"I see John has taken a liking to you," she says.

"We have a similar vision for this compound."

"Oh," she says and steps closer.

Her yellow dress, something I've never seen her wear, is almost the same color as the dried up blood I saw. It has frills around the shoulders. I place my hand on her frill, then let it trace the hem line in front, until it stops on the top of her breasts. I can feel my heart jumping. I notice the goose bumps on her skin. Why is she wearing such a dress when it's chilly?

I will enter her. I can't help it.

Just then I hear the footsteps of men. I step back. "Get me something to eat," I say.

She walks a few steps to the kitchen and pulls out what look like cookies. "The neighbors gave us some," she says, "isn't that nice of them?"

I take one and chew on it. It's sweet, almost all sugar, and it crumbles like soft sand in my mouth. James walks in as I swallow the food and step towards the door.

He pauses when he sees me, trying to register who I am, and what it means.

"Tom, it's good to see you," he says as he looks at me, then Samantha. It might be obvious from the crackling air what has just transpired, but I decide not to give him a chance.

"It's good to see you too James." I shake his hand. "What do they have you doing?"

"I'm surveying right now," James says, looking at me, then glancing over to his wife.

"I was just dropping by to see how things were going," I say.

He takes in what I say as if he will consider it more later.

"Tom was telling me how he's gotten close to John," Samantha says, her back turned to us as she pulls out more food."

"That's great," James says, looking at her back trying to read between her movements and words.

"How are the surveys going?" I ask.

He's busy staring a hole into Samantha's back when he snaps his eyes to me. "Well."

I know this means I should leave, but I want to at least temper things. After all, Samantha and I didn't do anything wrong, did we? "Where are the surveys?"

He glances back at me again. "Down south, we're trying to see if there's any rock that's indicates oil's underneath. That's the big push right now, oil."

"John was telling me this, that we'll be able to move the vehicles as soon as we find a good source. Of course, there's always the matter of refining it," I say.

My words seem to finally pull James away from the question of what just happened in his own house and to the conversation. "Vehicles?"

"Yes," I say, happy. If I'm here to impart information he doesn't know, he'll be more likely to forget what I may or may not have done. "They have a lot, some fuel, but the main thing is to preserve it for now."

James nods. "That sounds like the way to go."

"It does," I agree.

"And what do they have you doing?"

"Fixing computers," I say. "Or getting a local network up for now."

"That's interesting," James says, though I can tell he's lying. At least he's trying to be polite.

"Not really," I say. "But it will help."

"Well, we all have to do our part. This place is something else," James says.

I know how he feels. "They were definitely prepared."

"John was," James says. "They say God gave him a vision that the world was coming to an end, and he had to prepare, to make an ark of sorts because this time the Lord's flood would be with fire. And he was right."

This is new to me, and though it isn't that far off what I knew, it puts John in a new light. I wonder why he didn't mention the vision to me. "John is indeed a visionary man."

"He's more than that," James says with a scoff. "He's a prophet, a man who will lead us all to the Promised Land."

"I agree," I say, though the words seem out of place. I wonder if they'll believe me, or doubt me. All this talk about John seems very close to idolatry and isn't the same view I have of him.

"You've been with him all day. I'm sure that you know all about that," James says.

"I do," I reply. And then I know that James, and whoever he was with, has been talking about me. I want to know what it is that they said, what they feel. "What else have you heard?"

James pauses. "Nothing, just that."

It's too curt to be the truth.

"Tom," Samantha says, "are you going to stay for dinner?"

I try to look at her for only as long as would be polite, but I end up wondering what polite would be as I notice her breasts bulging, before I realize that I've stared for too long without answering. James shifts his feet. "No thanks," I reply then wonder what excuse I should give. "I was actually looking for MacGee, have you seen him?" I look back at James.

James shakes his head. "That man is no Christian," he says.

"Why's that? He converted today," I say, wanting to squash this talk. Doesn't James realize that enough of this kind of talk and MacGee will end up dead? "I saw it myself."

"We heard," James says.

I want to grab his throat and get all that he's heard today. Instead I say: "Well why do you think that?"

"He's too gruff. All day he was shooting down everything the compound did. He's trying to tear us down with his words," James says and finally steps away from the door and into the room.

"He was with you all day?"

"He was, helping us survey. If you want to call it helping," James replies. He seems so certain of himself, whereas I know that before meeting John he tended to be helpless.

"Where is he right now?"

"He lives a few houses west of the entrance."

I say goodbye and get a mumble from James who takes off his boots while his back is turned to me, and a smile from Samantha.

Looking for MacGee, as the sun dives to the horizon and the streets, or spaces between the shacks, fills up with kids returning from school and men returning from work turns out to be a hard task. Not that there are that many people, it's just that the houses are close to one another. I walk in the general direction of where the family told me to find him. I hope that I find him talking to others. I notice the sky turning a brilliant orange, shrieking across the sky. Another gorgeous sunset. Why aren't I taking the time to enjoy it?

"Tom!"

Sarah runs at me and jumps in my arms. I hold her and can't help but smile. She's out of breath and red in the face.

"What have you been up to?" I ask, spinning with her in my arms. She squeals with delight. Being able to pull that kind of joy from someone warms me up. I try not to think of the parts of her that remind me of Samantha.

"School," she says then turns to a group of children I assume are her friends. "See? I told you he was strong." With that she squirms out of my arms and runs off with the group. They don't run fast, but they do run with all their might.

When the sky turns dark gray and the night settles in, the lights come on and the streets empty out as quickly as they filled up. I walk by a couple shacks with their doors open and I see families eating. No one looks up to me. I feel like I'm back to the times before the fall where everyone was absorbed with their life and won't bother to look up at someone they didn't know. How could that be? Here in this flock we were supposed to be working towards the same goal, weren't we? Weren't we too small to be picking and choosing who we liked? I think about MacGee and how alone he looked. Everyone was picking on him. And for what? Because they weren't certain about his conversion? How fair or Christian was that?

A group of three teenage boys walk up to me. They have the badge of guards.

"Hi there," I say.

"What are you doing out?" one of them asks, the only one that's as tall as me.

I hadn't heard of a curfew so I cock my head at him. "What do you mean?"

"You need to be inside," the boy says, stepping closer to me.

I don't like his attitude, and his movements, like everyone's are slow. I step up to him so that our faces are almost kissing. "Says who?"

Another boy tugs on my antagonist's sleeve.

"Zeb, he's with John."

"I don't care," says Zeb, leaning his forehead until it touches mine. His eyes, in a dark shadow, are surrounded by a face that has a pug nose and curled lips. He wants to fight.

I think for a second then step back. I've heard the name before, but I don't recognize the face. Zeb doesn't move. I snap out my hand and he reacts. Slow. I grab the arm he's trying to defend himself with and pull it behind him. I don't want to pull out my handgun, so I bring my knee up to his stomach. The soft flesh I kick into doesn't feel human. The gasp as Zeb doubles over is extremely satisfying. I pull the arm in my hand as hard as I can and can hear his joints stretch. Zeb doesn't make a sound and goes to his knees. I kick the back of his neck, and he flies face down into the dirt.

The other two teenagers stare at me like I've done the impossible.

172

"What are you looking at?" I ask. "Take your idiot friend and get out of my face before you join him."

They scurry away, and I walk a few steps before I give up on searching for MacGee. I knock on a door. A man answers.

"Excuse me, I was wondering if you knew where MacGee is?" I ask. The man stares at me blankly.

"The new convert," I say.

"Oh... him." The man points down the street, then shuts the door on my face. The street dead-ends into the corner where the wall and the hill face meet. It's dark and no lights are on.

I stand in the middle of this unexpected darkness. The creak of a bed and rustle of clothes ring out.

Stepping to the shack where the noise comes from, I say in a low voice: "MacGee?"

The noise stops.

The door in front of me bursts open. "Tom? What the hell are you doing here?" MacGee asks, sincerely surprised that I should care to visit him.

I can make out his voice, but can only see the darkness of his form. "Can I come in?"

"You may," he says and steps aside to let me in.

When he shuts the door we're in total darkness. My eyes can't even make out the wall to my side, though my hand can feel it. MacGee breathes loudly, each exhalation is an expression of dismay, and each inhalation seems to be done with the utmost care. "Are you going to switch on a light?" I ask.

"Well," MacGee says in a whisper. "Why didn't I think of doing that? Wow, Tom's so smart."

I feel him brush past me. What could it be that's driving him to act like this to me, of all people? I follow his footsteps, the echo they make tell me that we are in a tight space. The place smells of old dust and mud.

It must have been abandoned before MacGee came here.

Finally we go through what I assume is a doorway. I hear MacGee stop, rustle in place as if he's feeling for something.

A match lights up; MacGee's hunched up outline comes into view. Some parts of the room do too: a desk in front of MacGee, a wooden floor plank, and a wall made of wood. I smell more odor; either mine or MacGee's.

With a lit candle in hand, MacGee drips wax on the desk before he plants the candle down in it. Then he pulls out another candle and lights that one, holding on to it. I see his bed next to the candle and his belongings strewn all over the floor.

"Do you share this place with anyone?" I ask.

MacGee points to his bed, I sit down. His face looks tired, his eyes red, and there is a specific energy that his features lack. It's as if he's been crying, as well as contemplating his demise. I want to reach out to him, to tell him that it'll be all right, to tell him that he can live under my protection. I don't. It could be decorum holding me back; it could be something else. But I don't make any effort to console him. I just wait for him to speak.

He half sits half falls on the bed next to me. The candle is in his hand and dripping wax over his fingers. He stares at the flame. I remember the encouragement and the friendly ear he gave me. That was a different time though, wasn't it? With the family there was nothing to worry about, no other interactions with humans—the family not withstanding—to interfere. Here it's different. I'm aware that being here is marking me with MacGee's taint. I wonder how I can think in such terms? MacGee is a friend.

"I don't," MacGee says with a deeper and more rusted voice than I remember.

"You're alone."

He finally looks up to me; his face doesn't even have a trace of the wit or sharp tongue that usually lurks on the surface. "You look well, oh chosen one," he says.

I smile. If he still has the energy for a tart remark like that, then perhaps he's just tired. "Thank you. How was *your* day?"

"What do you think? This place is nuts. All these people are convinced that John talks to God. Can you believe that?"

I let out some air. I would rather talk about something else. Perhaps about moving MacGee somewhere he can talk to people. I don't want to hear what he has to say about the compound because I like this place. And though I don't know whether John can talk to God, I do know that what MacGee thinks is that any thought of God is foolish.

"Did he say anything to you about that?" MacGee asks, his voice cracking a little.

"No."

MacGee looks back down at the flame in his hand.

I listen for anything that hints at the life outside. I hear a few shouts and laughs, but they soon fly off into nothing, and I'm brought back to the sounds of MacGee breathing. I realize that the candlelight seems so pathetic and small. Even here in this room it doesn't reach out and grab everything like the lighting outside. It's funny because I remember how entranced I was when I first sat outside with James and his fire of small chips. That could not have been much larger than this candle.

"Did they say why they stuck you here?" I ask.

"No," MacGee says.

I stare at the wax dripping down the candle leaving rivets in its wake and pooling in the area between his thumb and forefinger, where the base of the candle meets his flesh. The pool seems sublime, and it drips a line down the back of his hand, cooling quickly and stopping before it hits the bed. Every movement from MacGee changes the flow of wax so that there are soon several rivets down his hand. I notice his veins seem stunted. Everything about him seems frail.

"Did you like work?" I ask.

"No."

Silence. I wonder how much longer I'll put up with this, especially when he's not trying to reach out to me.

"I want to leave," MacGee says.

It sounds like the cry of a child. I try to treat it with more weight than that, but I can't help thinking of it in such terms. Has MacGee become a troublesome kid? And why does he want to leave this technological heaven? What is wrong with him?

"I'm not going to last," he says, still staring at the flame flickering in front of him.

I want to slap him, to shake him out of this rut. He's bringing me down with this talk of defeat. But why am I so angry with him? He's being picked on. I should, if I'm a good friend, help him out. I don't. Instead I listen to him move on his bed, staring at the flame, breathing like he's not expecting there to be air the next time he inhales.

I smell something foul, sulfuric, maybe ammonia. Almost like a fart, but not quite a fart—it's decay. MacGee goes on staring at the flame. Is he trying to burn a hole in his retina? I look at the wax, dripping, pooling, and dripping further down his hand. I'm reminded, in the flow of the wax, of the blood that leaked from Bill. From... What was his name? *Please... Don't.* I think of what I heard from John, how this group of people killed all non-believers. It's only because of me that MacGee isn't dead.

MacGee knows that.

Does he feel a connection with the other non-believers? Can he feel the ghosts? Not that I believe that sort of thing, but does he feel the dead people like him with his beliefs who died believing the way they wanted, screaming their last words before they passed on? Does he see this in the walls and the ground— those yellow splotches—and in the eyes and the sneers of the Christians around him? Is that what's sapping all of his strength? Making him into the ghost I'm looking at now? Did he feel like he's betraying someone, or something, by being here? How can he? He doesn't believe in anything, after all.

And even if I think that, know that, I also know that it feels wrong to push MacGee to deny what he believes. If I know what I feel with God is true, how will I feel if someone takes that away from me? Will I be the same?

The wax continues to drip. I think of what John did. It seems wrong and yet I cannot bring myself to say that it's wrong. Why?

Didn't I do the same? I did; I killed people. It had to be done. So John must have done what was necessary as well. Why can't I explain this to MacGee?

Please... Don't. I did that man in. That boy as he asked for water when he died. Jenny.

The look in her eyes.

What about Carol? Was my wife, the woman I shared so many sunsets with, one of those people who had been groping around in darkness, one of the people that John saw fit to kill? What if she'd survived intact? They would have let her live, right?

I also remember that before I was going to kill Bill he was about to say something, as if he wasn't surprised that I was alive, but that I was pointing a gun at him. I killed him because I didn't want to know, didn't want to find out what it was he was thinking. Isn't *that* the truth?

I am the problem.

I can't be.

"MacGee, please," I say, my hand reaching out to touch his, though I stop short, not knowing if I should disturb the wax. "Will you speak to me?" He needs to know that the most important thing is for him to survive.

"These people are evil, Tom. That's what the problem is."

"How can you say that?"

"They are. Maybe not all of them, but this entire operation is made for the purpose of evil."

"Because you think anything about God is inherently evil, right?"

"No. But I do think that these people are going to tear down humanity as we know it," MacGee says.

"How?" I ask. "Do you know that?"

"From what they've said. I've heard them laugh about the people they killed."

Maybe they were only doing that to make him uncomfortable; after all he was doing the same to

178

them, if what James said was right. "That's just talk, and that's just a few people."

"That's how it starts," MacGee says, finally looking me in the eye. "You really think all this is okay... good? That it'll end up fine?"

"I do. What about all the technology?" I ask. "This is the last oasis in the world. It's the only way forward."

"Technology isn't the only thing."

"How can you believe that? Everything I've ever read, especially by people who don't believe, tells me that technology is the only thing that matters."

I take his brief silence to mean that he can see the truth to my statement.

"It isn't," he says, though it's without any force behind it so I don't believe he really means it.

"Do you know what people are saying about you?" I ask.

"What?"

"That you're trying to be negative, to take down the compound from within."

MacGee shakes his head. "Of course they'd say that."

The candle is halfway used. I watch it flicker, threaten to die out.

"Why's that, MacGee?" I ask.

"I told you, this place is... not good. These people... not good. There won't be any good that comes of this place. None."

"And because of that you want to tear it down?"

"I don't. All I was doing was pointing out some fallacies in their train of thought. They were looking in the wrong place for mining for oil, and they decided to blame me after I told them it wouldn't work out." MacGee shakes his head, squeezing his lips together.

"They have it out for me, Tom. It's not going to end well."

"Can you not say anything? Just keep your head down and it'll pass. They don't trust you, that's fine, but don't give them ammunition. All right?"

"Sure... Fine. I'll be a good little boy," MacGee says.

"Thank you," I reply. "You will learn to like this place, I promise."

"Thanks dad," he says, but I know it's only to temper his acceptance of my words.

I remember that night we talked. "It means a lot to me to have you around."

"You too, Tom. You too."

I sleep there that night. The candles're blown out and only MacGee's heavy breathing to keep me company. The next morning I try to get him to cheer up, but he trudges off to work with hunched shoulders and downcast eyes. I think he might need some time to get used to the people, the place, the customs, and when he does he'll cheer up and jettison this attitude he's developed.

"Tom." John pats me on the back. We're in the great hall, and breakfast is about to be served. "How are things?"

"Well," I reply.

"Where did you sleep last night?"

I can feel several eyes on me, and I wonder if they know, if they think this is a reason to suspect me and my true beliefs. "I was with MacGee. He's taking some time getting used to this place."

John nods his head as if it's the most sensible thing in the world.

We eat the breakfast, bacon and eggs, and I try to focus on my plate so that I don't have to look at anyone's eyes. I feel like a traitor for conversing with MacGee, and I don't know why.

John takes me to the planning room again.

We're alone, again.

When the door shuts, John starts: "You've known MacGee for long?"

"Not that long," I say. "Why?"

"It's just that... you seem to be such a good friend to him, and I want to make sure that you're not the one being fooled."

"What do you mean?"

"You know what he's been saying, right?"

"The negative things?" I ask.

"Exactly, things that are measured to bring us all down."

"I don't think that's his purpose," I say, nervous that I'm risking my own skin for this.

"What do you think, then?" John studies my face, like he doesn't believe me.

There aren't many things that I can say. "He's a cranky old man who's probably scared right now," I say.

"Is that what he told you?" John asks and doesn't wait for me to answer. "Because I hope you're not..." And he stops there to look at the map.

I realize that defending MacGee might get me in trouble, so I stay silent. I'm angry that I'm being cowed so easily, but I think that maybe I'll figure out some other way to defend him.

"Do you know what these three camps..." He points at the black marks, "are composed of?"

"People?" I ask, uncertain and about the change of subject.

He smiles. "What kind of people?"

"Non-believers," I say.

"As far as we can tell."

"Right," I reply.

John nods, like there's something else he wants to say. But he doesn't.

A knock sounds out on the door.

"Come in," John booms.

A young man, one from the group I ran into bursts into the door. "Sir, we've found more people," he says.

"Where?"

"I don't know. One of the scouts just got back." The young man seems scared.

"Call the scout in here," John says. "Then call the council to meet here. Tell them to wait outside."

He looks at me when the kid runs away. "This is the moment of truth."

I want to ask him what he means, but there's another knock on the door before I can say anything.

"Come in."

"Sir," the scout says. He looks young, though not young enough to have a baby face. Dust floats off him like a mist, and his eyes, blue, stand in stark contrast to the rest of his body.

"What did you find?"

The scout walks over to the map. "We found a group of people, and..." The scout pauses to point out where on the map.

"And?"

"And they live in caves. They saw us."

"They saw which way you went?" John asks, a hint of anger in his voice.

"No... yes... They captured the rest of us," the scout says, his eyes darting back and forth.

"How the hell did that happen?"

"They came from behind, sir. We were surrounded before we knew it."

"What did they say?"

"That they would release the prisoners when they could speak about terms. They said we were acting suspiciously."

"How many?"

"Captured us?"

"No," John raises his hand as if to strike, and the scout moves back. "How many in the group?"

"We counted fifteen total."

John nods.

Within an hour he rounds up all the able bodied men, starts up the vehicles, and we stand with the entire compound in the great hall.

"People, brothers and sisters. We find ourselves in a precarious situation today," John says, his voice booming.

I stand next to him and can see how taken everyone is. The look of fear tinges the faces everywhere, but they slowly seem to gather strength. I feel excitement build up in my extremities and slowly push to my head. I'm looking forward to this.

"We have always followed the word of the Lord, and we have always tried to do the best that we mortals can do. But we find that sometimes the Lord will test us. And today that's what He's doing." John's finger points to the sky. "We have some evil men who have decided, without provocation, that they will steal our brothers from us. But we will not let that happen. Today, we will make a stand."

The hall fills with murmurs of approval, that cascade into a loud roar, pocked with shouts for blood.

John raises his hand and everyone falls quiet.

"Follow me in the Lord's prayer," he says. In unison the hall booms: "Our Father in heaven, hallowed be your name. Your kingdom come, your will be done, on earth as it is in heaven. Give us this day our daily bread, and forgive us our debts, as we also have forgiven our debtors. And lead us not into temptation, but deliver us from evil... Amen."

Three trucks start up, and rev their engines outside. The whole hall goes crazy and pounds out syllables as one, shaking the roof and the walls, and tickling my entire body. Like a massage of the soul it fills me up with energy. I can feel my heart pounding, and all I want is blood, blood, blood.

We drive out. I'm in the lead truck with John; the scout and MacGee are on the bed behind us. John insisted that MacGee come here with us, though I'm not sure why.

When we arrive at the place, the scout points out a cave ahead. Next to the flat land, right as the ground starts to incline are a few mouths in the side of the hill. We pull up a hundred feet away. John gets out his bullhorn.

"Whoever is in there, come out now."

He repeats, until finally a few men step out. They're armed, but I can see that they're scared. We have machine guns mounted on all of the trucks, and with all our men out, there are at least thirty guns pointing their way.

The men yell something, but we can't hear them.

"I can't hear you," John says.

I get the sense that he's enjoying this.

One of them starts walking to us. When he gets to us, John pulls out his gun and points it at him.

"What do you want?" the man asks. He's not big, perhaps even frail, but he holds his chest out like he's used to being stately.

John trains the gun to his head, and when some of the others hoot and holler for him to kill the man, he cocks the gun. "I want my brothers freed. Now."

The man nods, looks at me, then back at John. "Of course, there are some things we have to discuss first."

John pushes the gun into the man's forehead. "No, there's nothing to discuss. Let them go, or else we'll kill every last one of you."

MacGee is beside me, and he leans in to whisper in my ear: "See? What did I tell you?"

I shake my head because I know John has to act tough, otherwise these people will take advantage of us.

The man looks confused. "Do you understand what your men did? We came upon them when they were raping a woman from our... group. Do you condone such behavior?"

John pauses, pulling the gun back before pushing it back at the man. "Liar. My men don't do such things."

"Just ask the woman, ask your men." The man gestures back to the cave entrance. "They admit it themselves."

"If you've laid a single hand on my men," John says, his voice booming again, I will make sure that you pay."

The man again seems to be confused. "Are you listening? We didn't do anything of the sort. We found your men in the middle of a goddamn gang rape, and we stopped them and held them prisoner. We sent this one." He stops talking to point at the scout, "back so that he could bring the leader, you, here so you could punish them. We treated them, we treated them just fine, you can ask them that."

"Don't you blasphemy in my presence," John says.

I look at MacGee who raises his eyebrows.

"Okay, sorry," the man says. I can tell he's not sure what to make of John, and he doesn't know if he should go on with his talk.

I can see that John is looking for a way to push this man over. I, however, believe the man.

"Are you willing to come inside and talk?" the man asks.

"Why would I go in there?" John says, a sneer on his face.

"You have my word that no harm will come to you while you're my guest. That is our code."

"And what code is that?" asks John.

"Our law."

"Is it a law from God?"

The man shakes his torso to signify he could go either way with that thought. "Perhaps, but these are laws of men."

John stares at the man for a few seconds. I wish he would put the gun down. I'm surprised that the man has put up with it for this long. I know I wouldn't.

"Why don't I kill you right here for kidnapping my men?" John asks.

The man glances over at me, then back at John. "You could, but how are you going to take those caves?" He points back. "Besides look up there," he points further up and some heads several hundred feet above us wave at us. "We have trained snipers up there. And your men are in there and if I die, so do they.

"So they're hostages?" John asks.

"No... but if you make me one, they will become hostages as well," the man says.

I see John's jaw clench, a fine line drawn from his chin to his cheek.

"John," I say, placing my hand on his arm and slowly bringing the gun down. I look at the man. "Give us a second, will you?"

The man nods and walks off a couple steps and turns his back. He is very trusting, and I like that in him.

"How dare you defy my leadership in front of my flock," John blurts out. He's angry, either with me, or the entire situation. I can tell that he's not sure what to do.

"I'm not. Listen we need to get our brothers back," I say. "We can't risk you. So I'll go. All right?"

John looks at me, and the slight movements his head is making turn into a nod.

"Me too," MacGee says.

"Why you?" John asks, his face contorting into a frown.

"If they kill me, they kill me, right?"

"We don't want you to turn," John says.

"I won't, I'll just make sure these idiots give us back our men."

"He'll be able to help me," I say before John can turn down MacGee.

John looks at the ground in front of him. "All right, if you think you can get them to turn them over. But if we don't hear from you in an hour we're going to kill every last one of them."

"Thanks," MacGee says.

I walk over to the man, MacGee by my side. The man starts walking to his cave without looking at me.

When we near the cave entrance, I see the hostile look on all the other men's faces.

"I'm MacGee." MacGee sticks out his hand to the man.

The man studies MacGee for a second before he sticks out his own hand. "Thomas, pleased to meet you."

"Oh, I'm Tom," I say.

"Thomas," he says again as he grips my hand, like he'd never shorten his name.

We enter the cave and the men collapse behind us and follow us in. It's a large place, even bigger than the place I'd explored. The inside is lit by bare Christmas lights and naked fluorescent bulbs. I see dark holes indicating entrances to other parts of the cave. This main room has knee-high rocks in a circle around what could be a fireplace, though that wouldn't make sense.

"Your men will be here in a second," Thomas says, and jerks his head at one of the men. "You may have a seat."

I sit down, and MacGee sits next to me.

"I'm sorry about all this, but what your men did was out of order."

"You say you're a people of law?" MacGee says.

"Yes. What's wrong with that?" Thomas says. I think his moments with John has left him doubting our stability.

"Nothing," MacGee says. "I think it's great in fact. A law for and by men, right?"

"Right," Thomas says. "Do you want something to drink?"

"Sure," I say.

Thomas looks at another man who runs off into one of the holes.

I look around and realize that we're alone with Thomas. Is he really this nice? Does he not live in the same world I've been in? No, I remind myself, I need to stay vigilant; this could be a rouse.

"So tell me what happened," I ask.

Thomas goes through the details. They heard the shrieks from here and went running out to find our men on top of one of their women who had gone out to look for food.

"See?" MacGee says.

I shoot him a sharp glance because I don't want him taking a stranger's side. Nevertheless, I see that Thomas is telling the truth, that he might not be capable of doing anything else.

"You believe me then?" Thomas asks, eager.

"We do," MacGee says, and I nod my head.

"Good. After talking to... your leader I was losing hope for a proper conclusion to all this."

"Don't worry about him," MacGee says, a little too flippantly for my tastes.

"MacGee," I hiss.

Thomas sits down across from us. "I expect that these men will be punished?"

I don't know if I have the authority to speak for John, but I assume that they will, especially if they admit to doing it. "They will," I say if only to settle things sooner.

"Do you believe in God?" asks MacGee.

I want to smack MacGee on the back of the head so he'll shut up.

"In my own way," Thomas answers. "You?"

"No, I don't."

Thomas nods as if this is perfectly normal.

"We have a few atheists among our lot. Seems to make sense given what happened," says Thomas.

"Indeed it does," says MacGee, and gives me a look.

It feels like betrayal just talking like this.

"You guys been exploring your area?" I ask.

"We do. We've been looking for survivors ever since the nukes started to fall."

"What was your, your deal before the nukes fell?" I ask.

"Well," Thomas says and looks down at his hands. "We'd started a survival camp out here. You know getting people from the cities who wanted a taste of roughing it. That was our main income for a while, then we realized, as we got more and more calls that we could get money elsewhere. So we started a survival product line. It was big. You know with the gold bugs and all. Scooped in so much money that we didn't know what to do with it." Thomas shakes his head and gives a small laugh. "To think, I should've spent everything, and instead, it goes up in smoke. We actually had a few million in dollars laying around here," he says and points at the ashes in front of us. "But we realized that money makes some good warm fires. It took a while, but we finally caved in. Better to be warm and poor than cold and rich, I suppose. Suppose the gold bugs were right in the end."

"Can't burn gold," MacGee says.

"No you can't," Thomas agrees, though he doesn't catch MacGee's drift.

"And do you know exactly what happened before the nukes fell?" I ask.

"You mean why they were launched?" Thomas asks.

"Yes," MacGee jumps in. "He's always looking for a reason to the situation he's in."

I give MacGee another glance. For a moment I don't like what he's become, here away from John and the flock. Perhaps he does need to be smacked around to keep quiet.

"Well no one's certain. We know we got larger and larger orders for our survival packages," Thomas says and points at one of the dark entrances. "One of the biggest ones was from the government, believe it or not. And this was our storage facility. A highway used to run right outside. Perfect place to keep things cool," Thomas says and stops, leans back and lets out air in a dramatic fashion, his mouth cracking into a rectangle for a split second.

"The government? Which agency?" asks MacGee.

"That's the thing. As everything was going crazy we get this big expedited order, and I remember asking them what it is that they wanted it for... and the man on the other end says. 'You don't see it comin'?' Never heard from him since. Of course, all networks are down. Even the satellite phones don't work. A buddy had a shortwave radio and that too hasn't received a signal in ages..."

"No idea what set it all off, then?" I ask again.

"Yeah, it was a couple of generals, from the little bit of news that got through. They were these end of world types, and they were the ones pushing for a nuclear exchange the most."

"See?" MacGee says out loud. "See what I said?"

"But you don't know for certain." I throw out these words to dose MacGee's excitement as quickly as I can. I want to know the truth, but I also want to make sure that people aren't pushing their beliefs for no reason.

"No one knows for sure," Thomas replies. "Does it matter?"

"I think it does," MacGee says; he still has that grin on his face, and I still want to slap it off him. MacGee shouldn't act like this. At any moment, should Thomas choose, his men could jump through the entrances all around us and take us hostage. He seems nice, but I've thought that of others too.

"Then after the fall you found a lot of survivors?" I ask, pretending to stretch my back and glancing all around me to make sure that no one else is near us.

"You don't have to worry," Thomas says. "We're not going to attack you. Like I said, you're our guest. And yes, we picked up plenty of survivors, most of them blind, close to death or craziness."

"They all die?" I ask.

"Some were beyond repair. The rest we nurtured back to health. Still blind, of course, but at least they've gained their will to live."

"Blind?" MacGee speaks up. He too is looking around like he's expecting some sort of ambush.

"About ten of them survived. They keep to themselves, inside. They like the caves, I suppose. Doesn't make a difference to them. They've taken to burrowing holes everywhere. Even more of a maze than it ever was."

"You find most of these people out of Portland?" I ask, hope bubbling to the surface along with an image of Carol.

"No, Portland was destroyed. These were mostly people from surrounding towns. People who went hiking. We've absorbed about ten random survivors."

"Any other big groups?" I ask, my heart dropping back down as fast as it rose.

"Yours is the first one," Thomas replies.

"Suppose we'll be doing some sort of trade."

"I'll be glad to start some sort of trading."

I notice that the drinks, or hosting goodies of any sort, haven't arrived, and I want to ask more questions of Thomas, because he seems willing to answer any questions to the utmost of his ability.

Our men walk in with their hands tied behind their backs. There are four of them. They look the same age as the men I walked into back at the compound. I wonder if they have the same attitude.

"Here they are," Thomas says. "As you can see, we've treated them well."

I look at the faces, all of them facing down. The men look ashamed, but not hurt.

I get up and examine them. They don't recognize me. "Is what Thomas said true?" I ask, trying to boom my voice like John. "Have you disobeyed the Lord's law and taken advantage of a woman?"

The men stare further down at their feet; none of them wants to answer. It's probably not fair to ask in front of their captors, so I lean in to one of them and whisper in their ear: "Tell me, no one will know, just tell me the truth. You're safe now. I'm one of you. I'm with brother John." And I turn my ear to his face. I do this to each of the men, and each one of them admits it.

I step back and look at Thomas and MacGee. My head is spinning, though I try not to judge. There are several other men in the room, but I have no need to tell them what I just heard. Why are they going about ravaging the land? Aren't they supposed to take in people and help them? Did they give her a chance to convert, if she's a non-believer? I grab the prisoner closest to me and whisper in his ear: "Why?"

This one looks at me as if he is confused and whispers into my ear: "John told us... go forth and take what was ours. To multiply."

I shake my head. Misinterpretation. This was their excuse? "John didn't mean that."

The prisoner looks at me with doubting eyes, then back down to his feet.

"Thank you Thomas," I say as loudly as I can. "We'll make sure that their deed does not go unpunished."

I lead the men out and back to John. When I get back, I realize that John is left with only one truck. I take John aside, glad that he has finally decided to be more civil.

"The men did it," I say. "I asked them and they admitted it. All Thomas wants is for them to be punished."

John furrows his forehead at me. "Thomas is the name of the man who kidnapped my men? Of course they admitted to it, Tom. They were in the lion's den, what did you expect?"

I'm about to explain how I talked to them, and how they whispered in my ear, but John goes on: "Thank you for going in there. Thank you for the courage you showed. You are truly one of us," John says. "Though I never doubted that for a second. How was MacGee?"

"He was... helpful," I say.

"Well," John says. "Thank you for buying us some time." He pulls out a radio hand set that starts to crackle, and talks into it: "Are you in position?"

"Yeeess..." a voice said.

I looked over at MacGee who gives me an odd face. What's going on here? I'm not quite certain, but my body starts twisting and rumbling.

"Let's go talk to Thomas," John says the last word with a hint of distaste. He signals at everyone to follow him, and we all walk towards the cave entrance in a spread out file. I'm next to John; MacGee is next to me.

"Hello, Thomas. I want to thank you for what you've done for us," John says.

Thomas, standing outside with only a few of his men nods his head. "Of course, it's my pleasure. I just hope that such misunderstandings don't sour our relationship. We look forward to working with you." When Thomas says this he gives me a nod with his head. I look down. My heart feels heavy, my mind too.

"I'm sure there will be a great working relationship," John says giving me a smile.

I feel my hands sweating, but I don't know what it's about.

Shots ring out. They come from above us. A few single rounds fire off, a burst, and then everything is silent.

Thomas looks up, then back down on us. I notice John raising one of his hands, but I'm still taken in by Thomas' look. The man is scared and confused.

A sudden tussle brings my attention to the periphery where our men have guns to all of Thomas' men's heads. Thomas notices this too.

"What is this?" He glances at me. Though I try to maintain a stoic and calm demeanor, I feel an immense guilt and sadness come over me, and I look down at my hands.

I look up to see John step up to Thomas, and slam the handle of his handgun into his nose. The resulting crunch makes everyone twitch. Thomas collapses, blood trickling down from his nose, and looks up.

"Why are you doing this?" Thomas asks, holding his nose with his hands, his voice sounding like a child's cry.

I look away again. I will him not to beg.

The scout that drove here with us comes behind Thomas, grabs his arms from behind and picks him up.

"You think you can kidnap my men and get away with it?" John asks, pushing his head into Thomas' face. "Huh?!"

"They raped a woman," Thomas says, almost as if he has a love for these words he sees as the truth. "You agreed." He glances my way. "We agreed," he says, close to tears.

There is something definitely not right about this. I remember how I felt when that mother begged, the momentary rise in my blood pressure, as if I was programmed to enjoy such an act. I don't feel any of that right now. I feel as if it's my kindness to Thomas that got him into this mess.

I look over at John who slaps Thomas. "Shoot his men. Take the cave," John says.

Two men with huge backpacks, with an accompanying partner with AKs, four in all, approach the cave entrance. "Fire in the hole," one of the men yells and throws a grenade into the cave. We all turn and close our ears. The explosion goes off, and I hear a scream. It sounds like a child.

The men enter, and they send fireballs in front of them.

Flamethrowers.

The screams multiply and a burning man comes running out. All of John's men, except for MacGee and I, laugh. I pull out my handgun and shoot the man.

He falls into a heap and crumples up like burned paper. I look away.

"Good shot, Tom," John says, and I see all the other men in our flock nodding their heads. I'm still trying to figure out how to react to this... I don't even know what to call it. Does John believe that his men are so innocent, is this what it was all about—a sense of justice?

"Make him watch," John says, and the scout jerks Thomas, who is crying and shaking, and pulls him in front of the first of his men. The man is struggling and trying to break free and the shot goes off. A small red hole appears in his temple and he collapses, twitching.

"Stop this madness," MacGee says to me.

I try to turn my eyes elsewhere, but I can't, and MacGee isn't about to allow me to do so. He tugs my shirt. "Stop it Tom, or at least have the decency to look."

I stare at him. His eyes are welling up.

"You know this is wrong," he says.

"I don't," I say. I don't know is what I want to say, but the words don't leave my mouth. Another shot rings out and Thomas lets out a cry. John and his men laugh. The screams from the cave sound distant. The men with the flamethrowers must be in the further reaches of the cave. I'm trying not to think of the blind people being burned to crisps.

Another shot. "Please!" Thomas yells.

An image comes back to me, from the cold dark night between those boulders. When I press the shotgun into the man's neck and pull.

I stare at the scene in front of me. Isn't what I did about the same as what was transpiring here? The last man is shot and Thomas is shaking his head, rocking, back and forth. Everything seems like slow motion. The ground is soaked with blood.

"Well, I'll be the brave one then," MacGee says, and before I can hold him back, he is upon John and swings at him.

The punch connects with John's jaw; I hear the thud. John's head snaps back, he looks at MacGee like he never expected that. To him, to me too, MacGee is a defeated old man.

Some men pile around MacGee and hold him. I walk to the scene, hoping to save MacGee. What has he done?

When I get to them John kicks MacGee in his gut and MacGee doubles over.

"Shoot him," John says to one of his men. "I should have known you were a coward underneath it all."

MacGee looks up. "Your definition of coward is pathetic."

John punches him in the sternum.

"John," I say as I place my hand on the scout's arm holding the gun to MacGee's face.

"Yes?"

"A trial." It's the only thing I can think of to save MacGee's life. I may consider him a friend, but he *has* just crossed a major line. Even I can see that.

"A trial?"

"Yes, a new beginning, right?"

"Right," John replies. "Keep him with the other one," he says to the men who have their arms around MacGee.

I feel MacGee staring at me like I've betrayed him. I walk away because it doesn't seem fair that his eyes are accusing me when I just saved him, again.

It's only a few more minutes after this that the men with flamethrowers come out. "All clear," they yell with smiles on their faces.

"Great. How many were there?" John asks.

"About thirty."

John looks at me. I need to seem more helpful, for MacGee's sake. "That's the number I got."

"Good. Gather everyone," John says.

When the other two trucks return with all the other men John takes a count. We haven't lost anyone.

"Let's bow our heads in prayer," John says and we all bow our heads. "Our Father in heaven, hallowed be your name. Your kingdom come, your will be done, on earth as it is in heaven. Give us this day our daily bread, and forgive us our debts, as we also have forgiven our debtors. And lead us not into temptation, but deliver us from evil... Amen."

The prayer manages to take unwind my chest, allows me to breathe easier. I'm not sure why, but I feel more at peace with what just happened.

I don't say anything on the way back. In the rear view mirror, MacGee and Thomas run in the dust kicked up by the trucks, their hands tied to the hitch. Every time they fall, laughs rise up. MacGee seems like a stranger to me. Perhaps it's he who betrayed me.

I can't think straight for the rest of the night. We hold a giant feast in the main hall, and John even toasts my bravery, how I 'fooled' the enemy. I smile; I raise my glass, but I'm not there. When the dinner is over I walk around the shacks. People walk into their respective homes. I get nothing but cheery hellos and slaps on my back. Even the young men I ran into the other day see me and say hi. The man I beat down shakes my hand.

199

When the sun sets, the streets empty. I want something familiar, something from the past to ground me. I walk to Samantha's place. My lust rumbles, and dies out just as quickly. Tonight there will be none of that.

"Tom?" James answers the door after I knock on it a few times. "Please, enter."

I walk in to see Samantha and Sarah around their dinner table. They have some cookies on plates in front of them.

"Tom! Come in," Samantha says as she gets up and pulls out another plate. "So good to have hero here, right James?"

"That's right."

I walk in. "Thank you. Didn't know where else to go, really."

"Oh you must be tired," Samantha says, and I get that flash in her eyes as she looks me over in a split second. The air between us cackles. I try to dose it by looking elsewhere. I don't want to deal with that aspect of my life right now. Luckily, Sarah jumps into my arms.

"Tom. I saw you in the great hall next to John," she says.

"Sarah, honey, give Tom some room to breathe, I'm sure he's tired."

Sarah jumps down and points at a chair for me. I sit down and eat a cookie. It tastes horrible, and I know it tastes horrible, but I still chew it. It's as if all of that information doesn't truly register with my brain. As if my thoughts are to busy committing cannibalism in my head for them to worry about the signals my taste buds send their way.

"It was a great victory today, right?" James says, sitting down next to me.

"It was," I reply. What else am I going to say?

"They say that they kidnapped our men, five young boys."

"That's right."

"You went inside to negotiate with them, isn't that right?"

"Uh huh."

"How was it?" Sarah asks. "I heard they lived in a cave, that they were like savages."

I stop to think this over. It's hard for me to agree that Thomas's a savage. Did that even mean anything? "Well I guess they were."

"Were you frightened?" Sarah asks with her eyes taking me in with excitement and curiosity.

Who was I to cut her hope down? "It was scary," I say, and munch on more of my cookie.

"They say they were given a chance, but they didn't take it. They were lying through their teeth until John showed them what the Lord could do," James says, his teeth coming together when he finishes the sentence.

I didn't know what everyone back at the compound would hear about this, what story they would be told, but I suppose it's to be expected. And though I like being here, with familiar people, and I like that they're all regarding me with awe, I have half a mind to leave. I don't want to think about Thomas anymore.

"We heard MacGee betrayed us," James says, some relish in his voice.

I remember how MacGee had cut him down with words back when we were alone, how innocent that had seemed, and how that will now come back to haunt MacGee. "MacGee made a mistake," I say. "That's not a reason to judge him yet."

"I heard you said he should have a trial, in front of the people. The Lord," James says, his hand pointing to the ceiling.

"I did." I wonder what he's driving at. I feel defensive; the need to fight crawls up my skin. That need quickly gives way to the idea that I might lose my stature here with the family, with the other people in the compound.

"We think that's a great idea," Samantha says, reaching her hand across the table to touch mine.

I glance up at her, and don't see lust in her eyes. Just concern. Sarah doesn't seem to be much disturbed by the news about MacGee either. Didn't MacGee make an impression on them? Didn't they like him? Did all that mean so little? And if so it means my connection with these people, the family, the flock, means little. And if that's so then it could easily be me on trial.

"Him being put on trial?" I ask.

"Yes, to show him what he's done wrong."

I chew on my sandy cookie. I bite into a grain of sand; the explosion in my mouth reverberates into my head. I feel the sand grind against my teeth. I chew through it, and the resulting crunches send a shudder through me. Should I say anything to the family? Won't it be nice to get something off my chest?

"The important thing is," I say. "That a trial is held. That way we have the method of law."

The family hums their agreements, but I know they only mean to humor me.

"We're glad you made it out safely."

"Thank you," I reply.

"Let's give a prayer of thanks," Samantha says. The family links their hands on top of the table and I follow suit, holding hands with Sarah and James. I close my eyes and feel their hands in mine. Sarah's small, soft, and limp. James is rough, hairy and strong. I take in the smell of the room, the dirt between the planks of the floor, the cookie in front of me, the odor of Sarah's just washed hair. And Samantha. I can smell her from across the table. I remember her when she was closer, when...

"Our Father..."

I feel my heart pounding.

"Amen."

Holding hands, and speaking these words pours in me a sense of loving the family. We had a past, and now I feel one with them, with the idea that we are willing to sacrifice with one another. I think of God. I gulp and quickly ask forgiveness for my previous thoughts. I need to be better. Am I that weak? I think about MacGee. Am I weak for wanting him to go through this trial unscathed?

I listen to the family talk further about their lives, and problems. I smile and nod, and every now and then, I catch a string of words and ask a question about it.

"Sarah, you need to go to sleep. You have school tomorrow," James says.

"I should be going," I say as I get up to leave. Sarah hugs me then runs off to her room.

"Thank you for stopping by," James says. "I need to head to bed too."

He follows Sarah and for a second I wonder why. He must have sensed the air between his wife and I. So why allow us time to be alone? I turn and walk to the door as quickly as possible. When I reach the doorknob, I get a tug on my sleeve.

"Tom?"

I turn to see Samantha. I try not to look at her chest, poking out, calling me. "Yes?"

"We really are proud of you."

"Thank you." I fiddle with the doorknob as I think of what to say next. I remember how she and Sarah had laughed and talked to MacGee. "What do you think of MacGee?"

"It's sad."

"Sad that what?"

"That he would do that," she says, looking confused.

"You don't feel sorry for him. Hope that he'll come out okay?"

Samantha gives me an odd look. "He attacked John, didn't he? This is the way the world works, Tom. There are consequences for your actions. You know this. And MacGee is definitely old enough to know it as well."

I force out a half smile. "Thank you," I say and turn before she can fill me with any more dread.

Outside every shack seems to be turning to bed. I can sense the excitement of the won battle in the air. But the weight on my heart, my intestines, is too much to bear, and I know I won't be able to sleep tonight. MacGee. Talking to MacGee would be the best thing for me. He is the one man I can unload my worries on. But where to look?

The scream, muffled, raw, screeched by a person who has no other choice hits my ears.

I walk towards it. I finally get to the house where MacGee, the family and I had first slept. It's quiet when I step up to the door. I hear a whirring sound coming from the ground, and I wonder if it's the insects. It definitely sounds like an alien noise, something that hums in my ears and makes me feel like I'm in danger of being over powered by beasts. And, even though they sound evil, I almost miss them, because for a few seconds I remember the feeling they invoked and how close I felt to the others. Now, that feeling is resurfacing and I like this, because it replaces that unknown feeling that has been eating away at everything I have ever held sacred.

"Ahhhh!!" A scream cuts the air, shocks me back into the now. I place my hand on the door handle and twist. It's locked. I can hear talking, as if someone is discussing an intellectual topic. A laugh breaks through. Another shriek. I want to turn away. There can be no good in staying here.

I knock, as hard as I can.

My knock disturbs the people inside; I hear whispering; I hear the sound of a man trying to struggle. A hard thwack sound is followed by silence.

"Who is it?" A person asks.

Should I speak? There's still time to turn and walk back, or away. They wouldn't know then. If they don't hear anything they will most likely ignore it. Something in me, like a voice mimicking the scream I just heard, shrieks that once I enter that shack, I will not be able to turn, that I will not leave unchanged. The voice fights with the memory of all the good that MacGee did. There can be no blame placed on me for wanting to knock on a door, can there? I'm only acting on an impulse. Is the world ever a place where small innocent actions will turn upon the person carrying them out? Surely, that can't be. I swallow a tiny amount of spit, finding it hard to breathe. "Tom," I say as loudly as I can without breaking my voice.

"Who?"

"Tom," I say, louder.

Some more talking goes on in the background.

"What do you want?"

I think. What do I want? There can't be a proper answer.

"Just open up," I say; luckily it comes out as annoyed, and I hear the people inside scurry around.

"Hi," a face says through a slit in the door.

All I see are an eye and hair. Behind there only seems to be one light on. People move, like shadows shifting in place.

"Can I come in?"

"Why?" the person asks in a voice that sounds familiar to me.

I look around me. I could still turn around, but now that the door is open, I want to see what's inside. Think of MacGee. "I can't come in?" I ask.

"Not if you don't have a reason."

"I want to see what the noise is about," I say.

"Don't worry about the noise. We're only dealing with the prisoners."

The fact that he used the plural noun doesn't escape me.

"I helped to get them in there, so I can look at them," I say in a deep voice.

"Fine," the person says and opens the door. It's the young man I roughed up the other night. He still looks bruised up, but there's something in his eyes that tells me his spirit's at home here.

I step past him and into the room. An aroma of urine, shit, and a sweeter smell of blood hits me. I gag, hold it down.

"What do you want?" a man, one of the men from the main hall who was celebrating as much as he could, asks.

"I want to see. You have a problem with that?"

206

My stance works as the man shrugs. "Fine. Don't get in the way though."

There are other men who step aside to reveal Thomas tied to a chair, naked. His body, a skinny, wrinkled, flaccid piece of canvas has red and dark all over. His paunch, the only part of him that's not skinny, has a piece of intestine that hangs out. I see only the top of his head, as he's too weak to hold it up. He breathes fast, shallow. I don't want to but I stare and think about how nice he was to me in his cave. How nice he was to those prisoners. I snap out of it when I realize that everyone else is staring at me.

"Does John know you're doing this?" I ask, though it's to no one in general. As soon as I ask it I know it was the wrong question.

"Of course. He told us what to do."

"Of course," I reply. I step up to Thomas. He's tied down by metal wire. Where the wire holds him down, it has eaten through his skin, left the surrounding area bruised and in some places cut through his muscles. I see a quick movement flash in and out of my periphery. I jump back. Then, not wanting to look squeamish, I move closer to Thomas. Was it an insect I just saw? Will they eat him alive if he's left like this?

I look around. No insects. And even though I manage this, I feel my stomach pushing against my lungs; a nauseous feeling spills out. I look at the flesh where the wire has cut in around his wrist. There is black-crusted blood. I don't know why it's that color. There are open wounds everywhere and when he lifts his head up—the momentary respite from pain must be his reason to look—I see even more damage. His lips are swollen, and his bottom jaw hangs lower on one side than the other. Black circles hang around his eyes, both half shut. He is using a lot of energy trying to figure out who he's staring at.

"Tom?" he whispers. He's frightened. He starts to shake, making sure he doesn't move the wires. This means his torso moves, and his head. His movement is wavering between trembling and shaking, and his mouth is releasing huffs of air that could be him trying to say something or the birth of a cry. There is only one thing that I do make out. He's alone, and he's tilting his head like he wants a hug. He is desperate. How long has he been here, and how long will they keep him here?

"Doesn't he have a trial tomorrow?" I ask, still trying not to turn around.

"He does," someone answers me.

"Should he look like this?" I ask. I'm not exactly sure why I care what he looks. I should rip his bonds off and nurture him back to health.

"John wants his lies to stop. So he decreed that we purify him. That way tomorrow he won't lie."

The logic is there, but it seems wrong. Should I say anything?

"What can he even say?" I ask.

"He's coming around," the voice answers me and there is a smattering of chuckles.

I try to think, and again my brain blocks my thoughts.

I take a few steps back.

The men surround him like vultures. The young man who I roughed up the other night has a pair of pliers in his hand, and he immediately walks to Thomas and takes his nipples into the metal grip.

"Back to the cleansing, Thomas. Will you tell us how you kidnapped our men?"

I hear nothing but mumbles and shrieks, almost a foreign language, as Thomas tries to say something.

It's cut off by a hard and immediate scream.

I turn, the scream too loud and magnified in this small room. It runs right through my body, my heart, and vibrates my being instead of my eardrums. I did not know that screams could do this. In addition to shaking me to my core, the scream titillates my recollection of Thomas. Of how trusting he was. When that memory—the kind answers to my questions, the way he helped others—threatens to turn into a scream inside me much like the one that Thomas makes, I push it away. I try to remember how he took our men hostage, that just because a person acts nice doesn't mean anything. They could always be a step away from killing you. Remember Bill. And I tried.

"Tom?"

MacGee is in the corner. His is curled up in a ball, naked. His body, though wrinkled, and with a few bruises, doesn't seem in horrible shape.

"MacGee?"

"Tom. Why didn't you stop him?"

He has his energy, but it's waning. I wonder if they're going to give him the same treatment? Surely this is only something for an outsider?

"I don't know," I say, and I'm sad for MacGee because of the fear in his eyes, and I'm angry with MacGee for heaping more guilt on me.

"Why are they doing that to him?"

"I guess they..." I think of what to say. Is their reasoning valid? As it comes out of my mouth I realize that it isn't, and I don't know what to do with that information. "Want a confession."

"You know he was telling the truth, right?" MacGee tells more so than asks.

That's what I don't want to hear. Thomas, MacGee is talking about Thomas. But he could be talking about John. I will it to be John.

"Was there anything you saw in his eyes that said he was a liar?" MacGee continues. He's still speaking in a subdued voice.

I remain quiet. I want to help MacGee but I don't like that it means I will be tested.

"You know there wasn't. And he's already said what they wanted, and they are still going on."

This last part is punctuated with more screams coming from Thomas. From a break between two men I see that they are working on his other nipple.

"Is that true?" I ask.

"Tom..."

I look down at MacGee. He's staring at Thomas, and I see his eyes well up. I never thought I would see him cry.

"Why did you attack him?" I ask.

MacGee tucks his chin into his chest and pulls his knees closer to his torso.

I straighten out my legs. The fact that MacGee doesn't answer affects me more than I think it would.

I walk out. I think I hear MacGee say my name, but I try not to hear it, and tell myself that he didn't want to talk to me anymore. He did, after all, turn away from me. What can I do? A scream pierces my moment of peace, but it sounds much better coming from the other side of the door. I should not have opened that door.

I walk towards John's residence. I am not certain where I'm supposed to sleep. At John's front door two guards stand outside.

"What do you want brother Tom?" one of them asks with a hearty cheer.

That makes me feel better, until a distant scream sounds off. It doesn't seem to affect either of them, and I wonder if there's something wrong with me.

"Can I see John?" I ask.

"Sorry he said he didn't want to be disturbed."

"Is he asleep?"

"Not sure. What do you want with him? You can leave a message and we'll make sure he gets it."

"Never mind. I'll talk to him in the morning... Do you know where I'm supposed to sleep?" I ask, wondering how silly that question seems.

"You?" The guards look at one another. "You're in that one." They point at a larger shack a few meters away.

I thank them and walk to it. When I enter I realize that it's part of a complex of places. I see a central area that seems like a lounge area more than a living room, and the kitchen is huge. A hallway stretches out and several open doors with light and prattle leaking out of them entice me to enter.

I knock on one half open door.

"Come in," a soft voice says. I peer in and see three women, all young, looking up at me. "Oh hi brother Tom," they say.

"Hi. I was told I'm supposed to stay here?"

"Yes, we've been expecting you."

I see glints of something in their eyes. Part of me wants to forget what just happened in that shack, and another part of me wants to dwell on it, torture myself, because there might never be a better time to torture myself with what has transpired today.

"Where's my bed?" I ask in as flat a voice as I can manage.

They lead me to my bedroom. It's across the hallway and is large. It reminds me of a hotel room. I see a television on top of a box. I feel disgusted and tired. I lie down to sleep and women stare at each other for a second before turning off the light and closing the door. I can hear them talk next to my door, then silence.

The next day I wake up to the women chattering loudly outside. From the halo on the window I can tell it's at least midday.

The trial.

I walk out of my room and into the kitchen.

"Tom, you slept late," one of the women says.

I sit in front of a bowl of food and start eating it without answering them. When I'm finished I look up. "Anyone else live with us?"

They all shake their heads. I get the feeling that they're scared of me.

"Do you know what time the trial is?"

"Oh, it's in a short while. Everyone is going to see."

"You've seen one before?" I ask.

"No," they say. "This one is the first."

I take in the women. They're easy on the eyes. Was John rewarding me by allowing me the honor of sleeping in the same place as three beautiful women? For some reason just staring at them helps me forget about last night. Then I'm disgusted with myself.

Before my thoughts go further, a loud knock sounds on the door.

"Tom!" a loud voice says. The women jump, and a raven-haired one runs to the door.

A guard waits outside. It's one from John's door last night. "John will see you now."

I know an order when I hear it so I walk over.

I find myself inside John's house, alone with him. I notice a large red X on the map. I stare at it. It's the cave complex. I wonder if we could have learned something from them.

"Our first major victory against a foe," John says. "Thanks to you and your hard work."

The X seems like such an infantile way of marking our territory. And did John really think that I was thinking about backstabbing Thomas when I went to talk to him? Or was John trying to mock me? I take in his eyes, flickering about the map.

"Did we find anything of use in their cave?" I ask.

"Everything was burned up. They put up quite the resistance. We were lucky to escape without any casualties."

I'm not sure about John anymore. I stay silent, not by choice. My vocal chords have frozen up, as if they want me to know about the man in front of me before they go on.

"And your idea with the trial," John says, this time a smirk appears on his face. "That was genius. The power of a trial is never to be underestimated."

I flash a smirk back at him. I'm still not certain if he's toying with me. "Of course, a trial is what will help us move forward." I say.

"Exactly," John moves in one stride in front of me. "Then you do understand what this is all for?"

"I have an idea." I think, or try to think, it still seems beyond me. "What's yours?"

"That we use this trial to get the people to see something they haven't seen in a while. It gives us the chance to show that we're not barbarians, but will use the instruments of law to show people the right way."

213

And is law torture, I think? "The right way was from before the fall, right? The American way?" Something in me doesn't want to reveal what I feel about torture.

"That's right," John says and steps forward. In his eyes, the way they pierce into my eyes for too long, I can see that John knows something about me.

"And a trial, or law was one major way of showing the strengths of the nation, was it not?" I say.

"You're right to say that," John says, then raises a hand to stroke his chin. The way he does it, slowly, methodically, it feels like he's mocking me.

I hold my tongue.

"What were you doing in the shack?"

His voice is sterner. I feel like I've done something wrong. Have I?

"Seeing what all the noise was about," I say, and the calmness in my voice surprises even me.

"And once you saw that you decided to talk to MacGee?"

"Yes," I reply.

John examines me for a few seconds. "You talk to Thomas too?"

There's a smirk on his face. He likes this; he likes having power over people. Does he have power over me? The memory of me kneeling, looking up to John strikes me. No, that couldn't have had an effect on me. And yet...

"Yes, I did."

"That liar have anything to say?"

Nothing is ever fair. Is it? I remember Jenny before she jumped, then the feeling when I ran down to her body, hoping, dreaming that she was one of those lucky people that survives such a fall.

214

Of course she wasn't. Nobody ever is. And right now I'm hoping and dreaming the same thing but for myself. I'm hoping and dreaming that I will emerge from this the same, that I won't think about it, that it will just pass me.

"He couldn't talk by the time I got there," I say in a gruff tone.

"Is that a fact," he says more so than asks.

"It is," I reply and I wonder how easily I could kill him. I'm certain that I'm stronger than him, but will I do it? I'll be a dead man if I do. There would be no escape from this place. This is my world now. All of this is my world, and when I know this, I understand that I can't just kill John.

"Well, it's the way it has to be. For liars."

"For all liars?"

"For all."

"Why?" I ask.

"It's the only thing that purifies them."

I clench my fists, but I don't strike. "The trial, the law, is supposed to do the purifying. You know that right?"

"You're wrong. It's not the way it's supposed to work," John says. He's talking in that calm voice I first heard him speaking about his flock in.

"I'm wrong? You remember when we talked about what we saw? And you." I point my finger at him. I do it in a non-violent way, even lowering my voice, but he flinches back. "Agreed with me that we were to build a new chapter, something that eliminated the wrongs of the past, but carried on the strengths to the future."

"Of course, and I agree too."

"Then this trial matters as the next step we take," I say, losing some of my fervor. "The law, and facts need to be the things that people see, and see them as bigger than themselves."

"Of course, Tom, but I think you're confusing things. We need these trials to show people that we can take a step towards a new civilized future. But we need the trials to work for that. We get some belligerent in court, and we lose all that. You know this."

I don't know this, or do I? I may be stepping over a line, but I need to have it out with him. "Going that far with Thomas is not the way."

"Remember how even before the fall this was needed."

"Only in extreme situations."

"But it was needed. I thought we could go beyond that, but once we caught a man who escaped as a prisoner. He and a few friends had been attacking us off and on." John shakes his head as if it's a horrendous memory. "We asked him where his friends were, and he tried to lie. This is when I realized that some people's souls are rotten to the core and the only way to get the truth is to purify them. Listen, once we purified him we found his friends, his weapons; we were safe once more."

I'm looking into his eyes, his lips, and I can tell he's speaking the truth. "Only the pure tell the truth," I say.

"Exactly, me and you, we're pure. Thomas is not."

I don't ask about MacGee. I don't want to. John has opened my eyes to something I haven't thought of before.

I go to the trial with everyone else. I watch as Thomas walks forward, shuffling. Stretching my neck, I try to see if he has chains on his feet, but he doesn't. His face, as he passes me by, looks amazing. Either he has makeup on, or I might have been imagining some of the things I saw the previous night. Did I?

They sit Thomas down on a chair and leave two guards behind him. He faces the crowd. Behind him stands John and the council. Thomas shakes, mumbles, then trembles.

That is the same as last night. I look down at my feet. This weird movement and sound that Thomas makes, like a man about to cry but who has forgotten how, makes me sick to my stomach. The future. I think hard about the need for such things, and the need for such decisions by people in my position.

John has everyone bow their heads:

"Our Father in heaven, hallowed be your name. Your kingdom come, your will be done, on earth as it is in heaven. Give us this day our daily bread, and forgive us our debts, as we also have forgiven our debtors. And lead us not into temptation, but deliver us from evil... Amen."

I look to see Thomas shaking even more. A guard places a hand on his shoulder and he tries to stop, but it only makes his trembles seem that much more insidious and makes me breath hard through my mouth to keep my balance.

"Dear brothers and sisters," John speaks, booming. "We are gathered here today so that we may give an enemy of our beloved state a chance to confess his sins. Bailiff."

The scout, who led us to Thomas' cave, steps forward and reads a list of charges. They start out with gross disrespect and get worse. I stop listening after 'kidnapping'. I am, however, impressed with how official this all sounds. The charges, though plentiful, sound like something right out of a law book. Even the use of a 'bailiff' fills me with an uncalled for pride.

I scan the faces and everyone seems to be enthralled. I see sneers as people whisper to each other.

"Defendant," John booms. "How do you plead?"

"Guilty," I hear, but the bailiff repeats it to a spattering of whispers that rises up from the crowd.

"Very well," John says. "Then you shall have the death of a heretic. The final purification by fire."

Thomas, shaking, suddenly snaps out of it. The crowd is in a half cheer, but I can hear Thomas say, "promised... painless." The guards pull him up. I see him summon all his strength and lift his head, it moves side to side by a fraction of an inch. "No," he says and he catches sight of me. I should have looked away, but I am caught by the glare in his eyes, the last peace of energy that he has. It disappears quickly. His eyes glisten with tears, and he tries to say something to me. I think I hear a please, though I'm taken by his recognition of me, and his crying. This is not the right death for a man such as Thomas, is it?

I finally summon the courage to look away as Thomas is jerked out of the main hall.

The crowd gathers around the stake to which Thomas is strapped. I stay in the back, thinking about his last words to me. The flames rise above the crowd and I hear Thomas' last few screams. They seem less poignant than the night before.

I walk away before I have to smell him, or see the crowd cheer again. I hear them, though, as I walk into the little room that I thought was going to be the way I built the future. I play with some of the cables. I wait several hours before I walk back out.

It's still afternoon and I'm hungry more than anything. I want to go back to when the yellow splashes on the floor, the dried blood was only a theory. Not something that I had a connection to. Not a piece of someone that I had talked to.

"Tom?"

I turn and see the scout who led us to the caves. I look him over. I want to ask him about the burning, then decide it's uncalled for. It's comforting enough that he remembered my name.

"Hey, sorry, what's your..."

"Jimmy, that's what I go by anyhow."

We shake hands.

"You watch the whole thing?" I ask because there really isn't anything else to ask.

"Yeah," he replies in a hushed voice.

"You don't sound enthused."

"Am I supposed to be?"

"Your friends were kidnapped by the bastard, right?" I try to make it sound like it's a fact.

"I guess they were."

He looks like he has had a shower, and with the dust off, his baby fat is obvious. He's a child; he's just going along with this because he doesn't know better. That thought only leads me to think that if that's his excuse, what's mine?

"You guess?" I ask.

He laughs, then looks around. We are alone. People must be watching Thomas' charred body fall apart as the heat chips away at him like it would any other kind of flesh.

"Yes, I guess. Why?"

He seems honest, nice. Was I so screwed in the head that I couldn't tell the difference between the good and the bad guys? "No reason."

It's obvious that he wants to talk to me; he shuffles his feet back and forth and looks everywhere but me.

"What did you do before the fall?" I ask.

"Me?" He takes a moment to glance around then looks back at me. "I was going to high school in Portland when..."

"Where?"

"Tigard. It's a nice place."

"I've heard," I say.

"Was in my sophomore year when my parents went to one of John's talks... A year later we moved out here with him."

I could never have imagined doing something like that, especially as a kid. "What were your thoughts?"

"I thought it was nuts. I mean I was on the varsity football and track team. I was going to be all-state," he says with a zeal that I somehow find refreshing.

"Varsity? That's good," I say to keep him talking.

"It was. Had an awesome girlfriend too." He almost blushes when he says this, and I picture him taking harmless walks with a girl, making sure that he doesn't keep her out too late, and maybe even kissing her.

"Nice, hot?"

"Very. Better than these chicks," he says with a dismissive flick of his head.

I want to disagree, my cock does at least, but I stay silent.

"I was actually getting ready to escape and make it out to Portland when I turned eighteen. Maybe hitch a ride out, but before I did." He pauses to press his two hands together and then push them away from each other, his fingers outspread. "Boom. It happened. So I guess John was right in the end. Though he never said anything like that was going to happen."

"He was right, in a way." I look Jimmy up and down. He does seem more innocent than I thought. He doesn't seem like the kind of guy that can stand around and partake in, or watch, a gang rape.

"In a way," he repeats what I said.

"You still live with your parents?"

"No. I get to stay with the scouts."

"What do they say about all this?"

"They'd rather not talk about it."

"Why?"

"I guess it was traumatic."

"It must have been," I say. "And what do you make of all this?"

"I guess this is how the world works, right? You have to make a stand."

Him too. Everyone has to make a stand.

"You've made stands before, haven't you?" he asks.

He's right. Who am I to say anything? I had made a stand too. I had destroyed two entire families. Who am I to say anything?

Jenny.

The look in her eyes.

Please... Don't.

The splash of matter on my neck as he left this earth. Did he go to heaven?

Please... is what Thomas said. Lied to in the end, or he acted like he had. But a man in such straits would say that, wouldn't he? I had begged that family before they gave me a chance, and I shot them down. Jenny's look before she disappeared comes to me. Who am I to second-guess anyone?

"Tom?"

"Jimmy," I say as his form suddenly comes to me. "Yes I have."

He nods his head as if the world was finally starting to make sense to him.

"You played football?" I ask.

"That's right. Quarterback."

"We should play some games here."

"I don't think John would like that."

I stay silent again. I didn't feel like a man, or a human being, just a container for memories, and however I hold those memories, reacted to them, is what I am, or what people see.

The air feels stifling. I have to leave soon. I place my hand on Jimmy's shoulder. "When's your next excursion?"

"In a week. John told us to take a break."

I won't be able to stay in that long. A feeling of MacGee as he listened to me as I unloaded my sins on him. I need a release for all these memories bubbling up.

"See you around Jimmy," I say, as people start to filter out from the burning.

Inside my new home, I sit on the ledge of a table. My senses are heightened and I flinch when one of the women who's my new roommate walks in.

"Hi there," she says, flashing a smile. She's wearing a yellow dress that goes past her knees. The dress has what seems to be faded white flowers all over it. It frills at the top and is wrinkled at the bottom. Jenny. I push the thought away.

"Where are the others?" I ask.

She gives me a look that tells me that she won't be pushed around so easily. She slides in front of me, her hips brushing against me, soft. The outside world fades away, and I stare at her backside, barely peaking out from the flowing dress.

"What's your name?" I ask.

"Oh finally," she turns with a smile, her blonde hair, hanging down to her shoulders flies in the air and I think of Jenny, I can't help it. I stare into her eyes, a boring blue, a blue that reminds me of nothing; so I glance to where her hips flare out from her dress and try to imagine more.

"I'm Tom."

"I know. I'm Genevine." She smiles, crooked teeth not exactly spoiling the view.

"Geneveen," I roll her name out. It's the first name that I've heard that doesn't sound picked to be normal.

"You've got it," she says and turns back around. I try to place her age. It cannot be older than twenty. Blood is swirling around my head, my body. I feel a wind beneath my feet. This is better. With this sensation, it doesn't feel like my brain is cannibalizing itself. Nevertheless, it's still troubling. My cock is pushing against my pants and for a second I wonder if she's seen it.

"Where are the other two?" I ask.

"They're outside. They have duty with some of the surveyors."

I step forward, uncertain what I should do next. My hand goes forward, and she flashes me a look of curiosity.

"What do you think you're doing?"

I step back. What was I doing? Trying to forget.

"Just trying to..."

"Oh," she cuts me off. "I know what you were trying to do. I didn't mean for you to answer." And she lets out a laugh.

It's a decorative laugh that makes me smile. I relax. I remember how I was with Jenny on our first night. I would rather not do that and turn this woman against me.

"Very well." I lean back.

"You're giving up that easily?" she asks, again with the flash of her teeth.

"I..." I can't help but smile. Even though what I want is far away, I don't grow frustrated. "Did you watch the trial today?"

"What trial? Oh that. Yes, I watched it."

"What did you think?"

"What's there to think?"

"About the way it was handled."

She is fidgeting with a plate of cookies. They look to be the same misshapen cookies I saw Samantha dole out. She shoves the plate at my chest. "You want some?"

"No thanks."

"Don't like them?"

"No, I don't."

She tosses a few into her mouth and eats, her mouth open.

"You have no thoughts on the man being burned to death?"

"Of course, but why does that matter? You're the one who brought him in, aren't you?"

"Yes." There is no defense.

I turn and walk to my room. She hasn't provided the relief I thought she would.

I lay with my head on my pillow and the day slowly passes me by. Genevine hustles pots and pans back and forth in the kitchen. She peeks her head into my room: "You want something for lunch?"

I think of saying no, but decide not to say anything.

"And dinner?" she asks on.

I stare at the ceiling made of plaster. It seems rather overdone for such a world.

"Okaaay," she says and ducks out of my room.

"Close the door," I say, my voice low, my anger seeping back into my vision.

"Yes sir." She shuts the door.

I try to think of something besides MacGee. I think of Carol, the sunsets we shared, and the times we rolled around in bed. I think of Jenny. Her memory is more vivid, closer to home than Carol's. Why? Why did a woman I only know for a short while, a few days, stick in my mind more than a woman I'd known for years? Was there something inherently more passionate about the times with Jenny? I had sinned with her, and I should have been begging for the Lord's forgiveness. I remember the prayer and started to mumble it:

"Our Father in heaven, hallowed be your name. Your kingdom come, your will be done, on earth as it is in heaven..."

What did that even mean? We're back waiting for something great to happen, aren't we? I lose the thought as a tremble runs through my body and I have the urge to piss.

I can't stop thinking of the night MacGee listened to my worries and how perfect life seemed to be then. MacGee. I do not want to see him shake like Thomas, that is all I know right now. Wherever he is, whatever he's doing, I can feel him. I'm trembling with him, feeling his fear.

What does a man do when he faces his last day? When he knows the pain that he'll soon experience will play with his flesh and make him 'pure' and make him a trembling begging man where once a proud man stood? I know that we, this flock, stand on the side of the Lord. I had felt it that night when I prayed with the family. Yet what is Christian about the way Samantha dismissed MacGee?

I am thinking about this all wrong. We are building for the future, and the future cannot be had without a cleansing. That has always been the way, hadn't it? Now is the time for doubts to be put aside.

What had I done when faced with Big Lee's gun? I had killed him. Same with Bill. The family outside Portland. That had all been me. I can't point my finger at others when I am dripping with blood. It was needed then, and so it is needed now. MacGee tried to kill John. John is reacting as I did. Doing this is fine, doing this, making sure I live, is God's way of picking the ones he wanted to live.

This train of logic is gaining momentum.

Genevine peeks her head in at this time.

"Tom?"

"Come in," I say in a voice that brooked no dissent. She walks in.

"Shut the door," I say.

She seems uncertain, but does as I say. I point to a place next to me and she sits. If she had any rebelliousness from before it is gone.

"Samantha was just here," she says.

"Oh," I wonder why. I don't want to think of her. Her change of heart concerning MacGee still strikes me as vile. Though where that would place me is something I didn't want to think about. "What did she want?"

"She dropped off some cookies."

I laugh.

"What's so funny?"

"Nothing."

"I think it's nice of her."

I stay quiet. I don't want to talk about the outside world and lying here next to Genevine, smelling her, sensing that spot between her legs, is putting all my other worries out of focus.

I place my hand on her thigh and gently squeeze it.

She doesn't offer much in the way of resistance. In fact, she even helps me remove her dress, but once it's off she acts as stiff as a board.

I want to ask 'what is it?' but don't want to stop, or find a reason to stop.

"Say yes," I say.

"Yes."

It's a short moment after that, and I feel her clawing at my back, as I push.

The red spot that she leaves on my bed requires that I can't sleep there. She retires to her room, and I walk out of my home. I feel light though it is now dark outside. Outside, I see the other two women walking towards me. I turn away and speed my way to the guard tower. I miss the sunset.

And a scream pierces my world.

Nothing will make me forget now. It's MacGee's voice, all right. I must ask, I must face him. There is a lot of weight on my shoulders. I need someone to talk to, and MacGee might be the only person in the world for that. I make my way to the shack.

I step up to the door. The combination of laughter and screams now seems normal to me. I slam my fist against the door.

"Who is it?" a familiar voice asks.

"Open the door," I reply.

The door swings open and I see the same scene as the night before. Except this time it's MacGee naked on the chair. He looks worse than Thomas did the night before.

I take small steps and find myself in front of him. He coughs, or tries to cry—I can't tell the difference.

He looks up and takes a few seconds of squinting, and moving his head back and forth before he recognizes me. "Tom?"

It's a grateful voice. My eyes start to water. I look away so I can hold myself together.

"Everyone get out," I say without turning around, and am relieved that my voice doesn't crack.

"Tom, we have..."

"Get the fuck out now." I turn and stare at them until, one by one, they walk out. I walk up to the door and lock it.

I see a water canteen; I open it and place it on MacGee's lips.

"Drink."

He sips.

The wire hasn't cut deep into his skin—yet.

"Why did you ask for a trial?"

"I don't know." Instead of being annoyed at his accusations at me I welcome them. I want to hear every complaint he has against me.

"I've said everything... they wanted, but they still go on," MacGee says. He shudders, as if remembering something, and he starts to cry. Except tears don't come out; he shakes and dry heaves.

The connection between us is severed. Not because he's now an enemy of the state, but because of how he's begging, no longer a man, and how he looks. Can I help him? Should I?

"What do you want?" I ask, wondering if he still has the gall he had before, where he thought of nothing but his ideals.

It takes a few minutes before he stops shaking.

"I want to live... get out of here." He starts shaking again.

Can I do that? Where will he go? How will we live? "I don't know if I can do that," I say. "They will come after us."

He starts shaking, rocking the chair back and forth.

"Please..."

I turn my head away from him. Does he truly know who I am?

"Remember what I told you about the woman? The woman I loved."

I perceive a nod from him.

"Jenny," I say slowly. It feels like the first time I said her name in someone else's presence, though with MacGee in the state that he's in, I'm not sure if it counts.

He says something incomprehensible.

"She killed herself because of me," I say. I remember telling MacGee that she died because of her lack of belief, using it as a reason for him to convert. "She looked at me before she died; she looked at me with disgust." I feel my eyes watering up.

MacGee hangs his head.

"Before that, I killed a man, and I'm not sure why."

"Survived..." MacGee says, though I only recognize one word.

"I don't know if that's it," I say. How could any of this be about that word? What about the other word, God? I think of the prayer. I think of what binds MacGee and me. It's the very same thing that makes me want to shake with him, that makes me feel like my skin has wires slicing into it.

229

"Don't worry," he says and tries to move.

I realize that he's still tied down, so I walk over to where a set of tools lie, and pick up a pair of pliers. I walk back over and see MacGee recoil.

"No," I say. I quickly undo the wires biting into his flesh. He moves, but only a few inches. It's as if he's glued to the chair. "Better?" I ask, then feel silly for such a question. I notice a wound on his torso, part of his intestines peeks out.

"I'm going to die," MacGee says and starts to shake and dry heave.

"I know," I say. "I'm sorry."

He looks me in the eye. I feel my heart stop. This is how it will end. I won't allow him into their hands for another moment.

A loud knock comes on the door.

"Tom?"

It's John.

"Hold on," I say, since I'm sure they can knock down the door at any time.

"No... Please," MacGee says.

"I'm so sorry MacGee."

"No..."

I wait for him to say anything more, but he doesn't. Should I say good-bye? I pull out my gun and pull the slide back to make sure it has a bullet chambered.

"Tom, open up!"

"MacGee," I say, pulling up his chin so he looks at me. He nods, his eyes welling up. I'm not even certain if he can see me. I step back and walk a couple steps. I aim the gun. MacGee is shaking like he's beckoning me. The barrel of my gun sparks up. The bullets don't seem to do much. As if to answer that, the insects appear from the cracks in the floor, and I watch as they tremble towards MacGee and cover him. A weird nibbling sound rises up and the chair shakes. Soon I see nothing but bones. I avert my eyes from seeing anything else and walk to the door.

About the Author:

Nelson Lowhim was born in Tanzania where he lived for the first decade of his life. He then lived in India for a year before finally settling in the U.S. in the state of Michigan. He spent some of his formative years hitchhiking and hiking around the great state of Alaska. From there he joined the Army and served for seven years as an Infantryman in 1st AD then as an Engineer in Fifth Group. After his time in the Military—which included many travels through Europe and the Middle East—he came to New York and earned an undergraduate degree from Columbia University. He currently lives with his girlfriend in the Bronx.

Connect with me online (and tell me what you think):
Smashwords:
http://www.smashwords.com/profile/view/nlowhim
My blog: http://nelsonlowhim.blogspot.com/
Facebook: http://www.facebook.com/nlowhim

www.ingramcontent.com/pod-product-compliance
Lightning Source LLC
Chambersburg PA
CBHW051340020726
47501CB00007B/2193